misfits inc.

no. 5

misfits inc.

no. 5

the protester's song

mark delaney

PEACHTREE

ATLANTA

To my buddy BJ
who knows me well
and likes me anyway

A FREESTONE PUBLICATION

Published by
PEACHTREE PUBLISHERS LTD.
1700 Chattahoochee Avenue
Atlanta, GA 30318-2112

www.peachtree-online.com

Text © 2001 by Mark Delaney
Cover photographs © 2001 by John Fleck (U.S. flag) and Denis Chapoullie (hand on
guitar neck) courtesy of Stone

Book and cover design by Loraine M. Balcsik
Book composition by Melanie M. McMahon

Manufactured in the United States of America

10 9 8 7 6 5 4 3 2 1
First Edition

Cataloging-in-Publication Data is available from the Library of Congress

Library of Congress card number: 00-054857

E-mail the author at: misfitsink@aol.com

table of contents

Acknowledgments

Special thanks

to my dear friend
Gigi Tegge
who read my muddled first draft
and offered her support, comments, and questions.

to
Mr. Alan Canfora
for the wealth of detail provided by his website
www.alancanfora.com
Mr. Canfora is a survivor of the May 4, 1970,
shootings at Kent State University and now writes
and lectures on the subject.

to
Lauren Allen
good student
good kid
and perpetual emergency room patient…
for handing me one of the best lines in this book.

prologue

Saturday, April 11, 1970
Trenton State University Commons

Joshua Quinn picked his way through the crowd on the commons. A blond woman, her hair parted in the middle and falling past her waist, sat on the shoulders of a black man and held up her fingers in a V sign for peace. A pregnant girl of about seventeen sat on the grass playing a flute. Joshua saw someone scowl and raise a middle finger, but he also heard singing. The sun warmed Josh's back, and a breeze tousled his ponytail. A National Guardsman waved the barrel of his rifle at the man who'd raised his finger, warning him.

The crowd was not yet out of control, but Joshua feared that it could be. His skin tingled as though a charge of static electricity were passing over it. The crowd at today's protest was angry, and the National Guard was armed and watching. Last night a group much like this one had stormed the downtown, overturning cars and throwing rocks through the windows of banks.

From nearby a young man screamed something, his face contorted with anger. Josh couldn't hear him over the crowd, but he watched in fascination as the man's expression turned hard and his eyes flashed.

Luna aimed her 8mm home movie camera at the scene before them: A singer stood on a small bandstand, his shoulders hunched and his mouth almost chewing the microphone as he sang. His name was Dylan McConnell. Joshua had never heard the name before this morning, but he understood that McConnell was a "name" in the folk movement—that many believed his whisperlike voice and passionate lyrics would soon make him a major artist like Phil Ochs, Joan Baez, or Carole King. McConnell wore ratty jeans, leather sandals, and a long-sleeved shirt cut from an American flag. His brown hair fell to his shoulders, blending into the fullness of his beard. He fingerpicked an old guitar—one a little smaller than most guitars Josh had seen. A few scratches and dings marred its aged, golden surface. Even from here, Josh could see them—scrapes blackened by grime that had worked its way into them over many years. The round edges of the guitar, inlaid with mother-of-pearl, glittered where the sunlight caught them.

> I never doubted love or God or country
> I swore I'd lift my hand and do my part
> I sang my anthem, spoke my pledge
> I pressed my tiny hand upon my heart
> But today I hear the lies that all my leaders tell me…

At certain moments during his song, McConnell closed his eyes and his head swayed in time to the music. At those times, it looked to Joshua as if the singer were whispering "no" to all the images in the song: no to the war in Vietnam, no to President Nixon, no to the values of an entire older generation of Americans: Hatred of Communism. Unquestioning devotion to country. Were these so wrong? Josh wondered.

Joshua's T-shirt, which he wore under a Levi's jacket, bore the words Question Authority in rainbow colors across the front. Luna had bought the shirt for him. Until two days ago, Joshua had *never* questioned authority. In high school he had been the basketball star who always listened to his coach, the senior class president who smiled and nodded obediently to administrators and teachers. His three years at Trenton State had been much the same. He was a B-plus student, active in campus government, starting guard for the basketball team—a little short for basketball at five-ten, but quick enough and blessed with a killer jump shot and an eye for the open man.

Smiling, he squeezed Luna's hand and continued studying the singer on the stage.

Joshua had always listened to rock bands—The Rolling Stones, The Beatles, The Who, The Byrds—but folk music was so different. This singer stood alone; no bass, no drums, no electric guitar pounded behind him. Only one other instrument filled out his sound. At the end of each chorus, the singer blew into a harmonica

4 that hung from his neck in a wire-framed halter. The halter allowed him to play guitar and harmonica simultaneously. The two instruments, chiming together, somehow reminded Joshua of the dusty clay road outside his parents' farm in Georgia—and of his grandpa's hound dogs resting in the shade beneath the porch.

"You know what, Josh?" Luna asked. Her real name was Katie, but since arriving at Trenton State two years ago she had started calling herself Luna. She was new in Joshua's life, a romance of two months. "—I *hate* Nixon. I really do."

Josh nodded, not wanting to disagree. For months President Nixon had been saying that the war in Vietnam would soon be over, but it *wasn't* over. Two days ago the U.S. had invaded Cambodia, Vietnam's neighbor. Josh's number would soon come up in the draft. Now he couldn't put his hand on his wallet without feeling the weight of the draft card inside. Any day, he knew, the letter would come. *Joshua Aaron Quinn, report for basic training at Fort Campbell, Kentucky…*

Images played across his mind almost daily. He felt the scrape of the razor across his scalp, the slap of a folded uniform against his chest, the weight of heavy boots on his feet. Every night on the news he saw footage of soldiers lifting body bags onto helicopters.

The singer began a new song. The tone of the piece, with its sprightly rhythm and bouncy harmonica fills, was light and mocking.

Say, Mr. President, tell me why I'm here,
Tell me what I'm doin' with this gun in my hand
I signed some papers and stepped on a bus
Now they're sendin' me off to Vietnam…

From behind Joshua, several voices began cheering. Someone pressed fingers to lips and shrieked out a whistle. Several people screamed the song's lyrics and waved their fists in the air. A handful held up their draft cards and set them alight with matches. Joshua, uncertain about what was happening, glanced at Luna and waited for an explanation. She said nothing, only pointed the movie camera at McConnell.

"What's happening?" Josh whispered.

Luna smiled. "I guess you haven't heard this before. He calls it 'The Vietnam Rag.'"

After a while, I wrote my ma a letter
And I sent it right on home through Uncle Sam
I said, "I gotta go, Ma, and kill me a Commie"
'Cause that's what we do in Vietnam…

As the song went on, the shouting and catcalls grew louder. The electricity Josh had felt a few moments ago shot up a notch. He turned and was surprised to see how large the crowd had become. The whole time he and Luna had been listening, lost in the music, students had filtered to this area from all over campus. Two hundred, three hundred—Josh no longer had a sense of the size of

6 the crowd. The fliers sent out by the Students for a Democratic Society had worked. Many of the protesters carried simple signs and banners: a green peace symbol against a white background, a stenciled hand with two fingers raised in a V. Others held hand-painted works of art—a silhouette of a soldier holding a dead infant, his head tilted down in shame, or a field of wildflowers over which appeared the words War is Unhealthy for Children and Other Living Things.

"You're gonna burn your draft card, right?" asked Luna.

Josh laughed, scuffing his toe against the concrete. Luna had been pushing him, needling him for days. Not wanting to disappoint her, and not really sure how he felt about the war, Josh had done everything he could to avoid answering.

So mama don't expect me to come home soon

the singer cried

I can't seem to wash this blood off my hands
My uniform's torn, and the flag's all dirty
We're all dyin' in a jungle in Vietnam…

As the song ended, someone shouted, "Hell no, we won't go," and the crowd picked up the chant. Their shouts echoed eerily against the concrete buildings nearby. Josh remained silent, watching and listening.

Governor William Rose, stunned by the violence of the recent protests and the demonstrations that had shut down classes at the university, had called on the National Guard to secure the town of Trenton. That was the reason Guardsmen lined the campus commons even now. Three armored personnel carriers and several jeeps sat nearby, Josh noted; the Guardsmen, though at attention, glared at the protesters like snarling dogs on a thin leash. Josh couldn't hate these young men—any more than he could hate those whose anger against the war led them to shout and paint signs. Strangely enough, he felt—he *knew*—that he belonged in the center of one of these groups, but he had not yet decided which one.

Hell no, we won't go! Hell no…

The shouting put the Guard on alert, and Josh watched as they formed a skirmish line, shouldering their M1 assault rifles and readying themselves for the order to break up the protest. One of the Guardsmen, wearing the three stripes of a sergeant, grabbed a bullhorn and stepped on the hood of a jeep. "This is an illegal assembly," he called out. "You are ordered to disperse."

Before the sergeant even finished speaking, a bottle arced through the air, whirling in seeming slow motion before smashing into a diamond spray against the grill of the sergeant's jeep. The crowd of protesters began shouting louder. *Hell no, we won't go! Hell no, we won't go!* Luna let go of Josh's hand. She hurled a rock at one of the Guardsmen and screamed an obscenity when it bounced off his helmet.

8

Then she was gone.

The crowd surged forward, and Josh lost her. In the sudden scuffle, and with the bodies pressed against him, he saw only a whirlwind of images: the scowling face of a young woman, a clenched fist, a dazed man wiping blood from a cut above the eye. Moments later Josh heard a sudden loud puff of air, and the sound repeated itself—*shoof, shoof, shoof, shoof!* Canisters the size of soup cans fell from the sky and landed among the protesters. The canisters trailed plumes of smoke. At first Josh didn't understand what had happened, but then he knew. The Guard had fallen back and were lobbing tear gas into the crowd.

Tufts of white fog billowed from the ground where the canisters landed. Josh felt a stinging, then a searing sensation in his eyes and nose. The spring breeze dissipated the gas quickly, but not quickly enough. When Josh could make out the other protesters, he saw that most already had glistening red eyes and tears streaming down their cheeks. Several tore past him, hands or jackets clamped over their faces. Josh wanted to run too, but Luna—where was Luna? He looked for her, blinking helplessly and rubbing his eyes, but seeing only a blurred image of the Guardsmen marching back toward him, ready to finish the job the tear gas had started.

Luna...

As Josh turned, one of the National Guard jeeps exploded in a burst of orange and yellow flame. Josh saw the fireball, then felt a wall of hot air slam into him and lift him off his feet, tossing him against a tree. A second explosion followed—muffled this time by a pain and ringing in Josh's ears—and then a third. Josh felt something like needles, dozens of them, stabbing into his leg, and he watched as the hood of one of the jeeps flew over his head, blackened and trailing flames. He slid to the ground, the leg of his jeans suddenly heavy and wet.

Strangely, the pain in his leg faded. After a few moments the leg began to feel numb, then it turned icy cold. That was a good sign, wasn't it—no pain? Two Guardsmen ran up to Josh and leaned over him. He saw their mouths moving but couldn't hear what they were saying. He tried to talk to them, to tell them he was all right, but he couldn't think. His head ached so. One of the Guardsmen held a handkerchief to Josh's ear, and it came away smeared with blood. The other Guardsman peeled off his uniform shirt and began wrapping it around the injured leg. No, Josh thought, not quite able to force out the words, *I'm all right. Really. Where's Luna?* The coldness in his leg began to spread throughout his entire body, and Josh shivered.

His vision, which had been faintly blurred, came into a little better focus. He looked around—at the group of protesters a hundred or so yards away, at the three burning jeeps—then his gaze fell once again on the singer. For a moment McConnell stared down at him. Josh saw a faint bobbing in the singer's throat as he swallowed, and the man's gaze was wide and unbelieving. He started shaking his head as he had while singing; it was that same motion, Josh remembered: *no...no...no...* Then

10 the man threw his guitar into its case, snapped the latches, and ran.

Josh felt several pairs of arms lift him onto a stretcher. He stared up at the sky, past the faces of the men looking down at him. One of the men spoke, but Josh couldn't hear what he was saying. His thoughts were on the singer, Dylan McConnell.

It was you, wasn't it, Josh thought. *You're the man who did this to me…*

From inside the ambulance, the siren sounded faint and very far away.

chapter one

One Tuesday, thirty years later...

Jake Armstrong's clarinet sang across the Bugle Point High School band room as it never had before. Later this afternoon Jake would have his marching band class, with all its high-stepping and chunky rhythms. This, however, was jazz band, where the music was more bluesy and sensual, and where notes sometimes slid around as though they weren't sure where they belonged on the staff.

The song was "Chattanooga Choo-Choo." Jake closed his eyes and geared up for his favorite part, a section where he, as first clarinet, had a lengthy solo. Furthermore, because this was jazz, Jake could improvise. He followed the rhythm and the song's chord structure, but within those confines he could play *anything*. It was time. Jake leaned back and angled his horn toward the ceiling, finding notes that snaked around the song's melody without actually hitting it. As he reached the end

12 of the solo, he punched out the last measure and grinned as the saxophone took over.

Mr. Janson pointed his baton directly at the sax player, but glanced at Jake with a faint smile. Patty Arbour, the freshman girl who sat next to Jake, struggled to put her retainer back in now that the song was coming to a close. She nodded at him and whispered, "That was *eckthallent*."

Jake acknowledged the compliment with a nod. When band class ended, he pulled his clarinet apart and laid it gently into its case, adjusting the ebony pieces against the crushed velvet lining.

He smiled. Beyond the thrill of playing jazz, beyond Patty's compliment and the look from Mr. Janson—beyond, even, his magnificent antique clarinet—Jake had another thought on his mind. Today, for the first time, he would beat little Mattie Ramiro at his own game. For over a year now, Mattie had driven Jake crazy with his ability to worm his way in and out of Jake's school day. Notes magically appeared in Jake's locker, even though Jake's padlock required a key and Mattie never asked for it. Other times a slip of paper would appear under the cover of Jake's literature book, though Jake would have just arrived at school—with the lit book in hand—and hadn't even seen Mattie. More than once Jake had even found a note curled inside his clarinet case—*his clarinet case!*—an object he rarely let out of his hands and never out of his sight. Jake hadn't a clue how Mattie accomplished these mysterious doings, but today he was going to pay Mattie back for every one of them. He had waited for this moment. He had planned for it. He was ready.

Earlier this morning, Jake's friend, Byte Salzmann, had approached Jake with three notes, asking him to deliver one to each member of their group. Usually Mattie was the one chosen to play mailman, since he had this almost supernatural knack for locating the others, but Byte had been too impatient to hunt down the elusive boy. Instead she had run up to Jake, bouncing on the balls of her feet and waving her arms. "Here!" she had said, thrusting the notes into Jake's huge palm. "Get these to the others, okay?" Then she had waved her arms again, spun around, and run off to first period.

Jake slipped the notes from his pocket now and examined them. Folded into quarters, each slip of paper bore an odd symbol—a circle overlapping and intersecting a square. It was the emblem Jake and his friends had chosen for themselves, the sign of the Misfits. The geometric pattern represented a square peg and a round hole, two shapes that could never fit together. *And isn't that the truth,* Jake thought. Jake stared at the emblem and recalled how he had once tried out for football. It had seemed such a natural choice. Jake was six feet two inches tall and a muscular two hundred pounds, quick and graceful on his feet. Yet on the practice field he soon discovered that he hated the in-your-face aggression of the sport. Similarly, each of his friends—Peter, Byte, and Mattie—had learned that high school was a place where

14 teens discovered who they were by experimenting with different activities. *But what do you do,* Jake wondered, *when the You you discover is different from the You everyone else thinks you should be?* The high school world demanded certain likes, certain dislikes, certain values. What if you were *different?*

With first period winding to a close, Jake now unfolded the note bearing his name and began to read. The message from Byte was short and simple, and it made Jake smile even more. *Way to go,* he thought. He would see Peter between classes and would pass along the message then.

Mattie, Jake mused, was a separate challenge entirely.

When the bell rang, Jake gathered up his clarinet, his band jacket, and his schoolbooks and slipped through the rear door of the band room. He took a different path from his usual one, so that he headed not into the English wing, where Mattie would certainly run into him, but rather into the main sophomore hallway where the tenth-grade lockers lined the walls. Jake, like many band students, kept his books in his band locker, which meant he provided his own lock. Mattie, however, used a regular student locker that had a built-in combination. The front office kept the combinations on file and changed them out every summer, so students couldn't get into lockers they'd been assigned in previous years. The system appeared quite secure.

Jake grinned with an almost evil satisfaction. The system, he thought, *was* secure—unless, of course, a fellow band student worked as an aide in the office. In that case, Jake had discovered, one could acquire another student's locker combination with a handful of two-for-one sandwich coupons from the nearby Subway.

Jake shouldered his way through the crowded corridor, knowing full well that he had only the five-minute passing period to complete his mission and get to his next class. Mattie's second period was all the way in the E wing, so Jake figured his friend wouldn't have the time to make a locker stop now. Everything was perfect.

1024, he counted to himself, *1026, 1028…* There it was—*1032.* Mattie's locker. Jake dug into his jacket pocket and pulled out a rumpled slip of paper. As he did, his heart began to beat faster. A flash of paranoia made him glance around one last time before staring down at the scrawled combination. *37…13…26…* He fumbled a couple of times, moving past the numbers, getting mixed up over whether the turn should be clockwise or counter-clockwise, but after a few moments he stopped and stared at the dial. It rested perfectly on the number 26.

Jake took a deep breath and tugged upward on the chrome handle. The door popped open with a squeal loud enough to startle him. He opened the door wide but slowly now, wincing as it creaked.

Before him were Mattie's schoolbooks and a rumpled sweater. On top of these lay a brown paper bag that might have been Mattie's lunch but instead contained the disassembled remains of an analog clock radio, a digital tuner from a Walkman stereo, and a Dolly Madison

16   cupcake crushed in its wrapper, surrounded by a smear of exploded filling.

Jake grinned. Now came the fun part. He took out the paper bag and the sweater and reached for the cover of Mattie's French book. Jake's plan was to place the note under the book's cover, so Mattie would know that Jake had not merely walked by and stuffed it through the locker's vents. When Mattie got to third period, he would find the note "magically" tucked within his French lesson. Jake nodded in satisfaction at the image this brought to mind: Mattie fuming, tearing at the note as he opened it, grumbling at being beaten at his own trick.

Jake slipped Byte's note from his pocket and smoothed it out. Still smiling, he lifted the cover of Mattie's French book and readied himself to place it there.

And in an instant his smile melted away.

A sheet of notebook paper, folded in half so its edges didn't peek from beyond the book cover, stared up at him. Huge letters written in Mattie's trademark scrawl spelled out a simple message...

Turn around, Jake.

Jake tilted his head slightly, hoping the note might make more sense if he viewed it from a different angle. It didn't.

"What part of it don't you understand?" asked a familiar voice.

At the sound of the voice, the sweater and bag of electronic parts seemed to leap from Jake's fingers. They fell to the floor, the bag clattering as it struck the linoleum.

Jake scooped the mess up and spun around, clutching the bag and the sweater in a crumpled ball against his chest. Facing him, close enough to reach up and tap him on the shoulder, was a brown-haired boy who stood no taller than four feet eleven and who weighed less than a hundred pounds.

"You have the technique," said Mattie Ramiro, "but none of the style." He pointed at the bag of electronics. "And be careful with that. You could break something."

Jake stuffed Mattie's belongings back into the locker and slammed the door shut. He then handed Mattie the note Byte had written. "Okay," he said, surrendering, "how did you know?"

Mattie unfolded Byte's note with one hand and began reading. As he did, he reached with the other hand into the pocket of his jean jacket and pulled out a fistful of Subway coupons. "Here," he said, never taking his eyes off the note. "He likes TCBY better." He read for another moment or two, then refolded the note and tucked it away. "So she did it, huh?"

Jake, still embarrassed at having been caught, nodded instead of speaking.

"You realize then," continued Mattie, "that our lives are in danger?"

Jake snorted with as much good humor as he could muster. "Come on," he said, "we'll be late to class."

They walked along the corridor, Jake occasionally turning sideways to pass through the clusters of people, Mattie slipping in and out like a phantom. Though Jake stood very near to Mattie, even talking to him as they moved, he still found it difficult to fathom how the younger boy managed it.

"How do you do that?" he asked.

Mattie stopped walking and stared up at Jake. Without a word he took Jake's notebook from his hand and tore out a sheet of paper. He handed the sheet to Jake. "Write your name on that," he ordered.

Jake, frowning, took out a pen and scribbled his name across the paper.

"Now tear it up," said Mattie.

Jake tore the sheet into several pieces. Mattie took them and crumpled them in his fist. He held the fist up so Jake could see his tightly clenched fingers up close. Then he turned his hand upside down, dumped the paper into Jake's palm, and continued walking.

"Wha...?" said Jake.

He gazed at the crumpled mass in his hand and, not exactly sure what Mattie wanted him to do, slowly pulled at it. But the paper didn't fall apart as he expected. In fact, he now saw a piece that he was certain was larger than any of the ones he had torn. He kept pulling at the wad, unbelieving, until the obvious—and the impossible—became clear.

The paper was no longer torn at all. It was one piece, crumpled but otherwise undamaged. In the center, in Jake's huge scribble, was his name, just as he had written it. Below that were four tiny words, written in Mattie's handwriting: *See you after school.*

Jake looked down the corridor. "Mattie!" he roared. But Mattie had vanished.

The balled-up sheet of notebook paper hurtled across the library and bounced off Peter Braddock's right ear. He watched it hit the floor and scuttle like a bug beneath the table. Peter rubbed his ear and gritted his teeth. Two other balled-up sheets lay scattered nearby, and he'd had just about enough.

Determined to put an end to the paper throwing, Peter glared across the library at his number one suspect. Three tables away sat Justin Ingler. Justin, Peter knew, was a Class A troublemaker. Sometimes Justin took marking pens and drew pictures on his forearms: a skull with a sword passing through it, a dragon with blood dripping from its fangs, a smiley face with a bullet hole between the eyes. Then he'd proclaim to his friends he had gotten a tattoo. He was the kind of troublemaker one almost pitied.

Justin leaned over a sheet of paper—no doubt a blank one—with a frown of concentration wrinkling his forehead. He glanced up at Peter and grinned evilly, but only for an instant, just long enough to take credit for the paper wads. The grin then quickly dissolved into a blank, questioning stare: *What? Me?* It was just enough of a confession to satisfy Peter that a little payback was in order. He filed the thought away and went back to work.

Justin Ingler chuckled.

20   Mrs. Forrestal had brought her entire English class into the library this morning to do research, so for the next twenty minutes, Peter gathered materials for his project on Edgar Allen Poe. He found an online article on Poe's life, a Poe biography on the library shelf, and several magazine photos of the Poe House in New York, which he would use as a visual aid for the oral presentation his English teacher had assigned.

Peter forgave Mrs. Forrestal for not catching the paper throwing. He didn't know how old his English teacher was, but he knew from last year's annual that Mrs. Forrestal's first name was Bertha, which meant she came from a generation when names like Bertha were considered attractive.

Ms. Langley, the librarian, smiled as he brought the biography up to the checkout counter. "Having a good day, Peter?" she asked. She glanced at Justin as she spoke, suggesting that she suspected him of pulling some nonsense but had not actually witnessed anything.

Peter smiled back. "I'm having a wonderful day, thank you," he said. "Couldn't be better."

Ms. Langley gazed at him quizzically as she ran the laser pen across the bar codes on Peter's library card and the back of the book.

Turning from the counter, Peter noted that Justin Ingler had actually gotten off his rear and gone over to the magazine section. In Peter's pocket was a small, copper-wound magnet left over from a recent project in his science class. Peter dug it out and stared at it as it rolled around in his palm. Justin Ingler's backpack lay open just two tables away.

Peter walked over and lifted the flap to gaze inside the backpack. *Pretty much what I'd expect,* he mused. The pack contained several loose sticks of gum, a bottle of what looked like diarrhea medicine, and two magazines whose covers alone made Peter's face turn bright red with embarrassment. Checking to make sure Ingler—and Ms. Langley—couldn't see him, Peter dropped the magnet inside the pack and calmly returned to his table.

He wanted to get right back to work, but Byte's note stared up at him from the tabletop. Jake had given it to him earlier in the day, and though Peter could guess what it said even before he had read it, the note still made him smile. He picked it up now, tapping it against his palm and thinking of the celebration that would come later.

The hiss of the library door interrupted Peter's thoughts. Mr. Steadham, the new principal, walked in and nodded a terse greeting to Ms. Langley. The librarian stiffened. She nodded back, but slowly, and her face paled as she did. Mr. Steadham walked past her and strode toward the fiction shelves that lined the library walls.

Peter closed his book and watched.

His father, Nick Braddock, was a special agent for the FBI. Peter had long ago learned—or perhaps inherited—his father's skill at observation and deduction. Peter ran some facts through his mind: Mr. Steadham, in his short time at the high school, was not known for frequenting the library. Peter more often saw the principal behind his desk in the administration office, or wandering the outer yard during lunch, slapping students on the shoulder to say hello and telling others to stand up straight or tuck their shirts in. He was a thickly built, balding man who seemed more suited to a football field, Peter thought, than an administrator's office.

Ms. Langley fidgeted in the principal's presence. Peter had always known Ms. Langley to be strong but friendly in her dealings with students and faculty. More than once he had seen her verbally shred a student for some infraction, then watched in fascination as she had that very same student laughing at one of her jokes as he made his way to the vice-principal's office for an in-school suspension. Yet she remained oddly stiff now, and Peter noted that her hands were shaking.

Peter turned his attention back to the principal. Mr. Steadham moved from shelf to shelf, pulling off books here and there, occasionally referring to a sheet of paper in his hand. He removed five or six books from the fiction area, then strode to the nonfiction section and removed several more. When his arms were full, he dropped the books onto a rolling cart and wheeled them past the checkout desk. Peter could see a few of the titles: *Slaughterhouse-Five; The Catcher in the Rye; Johnny Got His Gun; Are You There God? It's Me, Margaret.*

"I believe these are the titles we discussed," he said to Ms. Langley.

"Mr. Steadham," Ms. Langley whispered, "I really must object to this. As a librarian, I have a duty to…" She stammered, almost spitting the words. "I mean…those books…" The principal smiled at Ms. Langley, but the smile reminded Peter of an animal baring its fangs. "Your concern is noted," Steadham said flatly, "but the school board has made its decision."

As Mr. Steadham wheeled the books past Ms. Langley, she grasped the cart, her fingers tightening around the handle. She stepped up to Mr. Steadham, then glanced around the library to make sure that students were occupied with their work and not her conversation. Peter looked down and pretended to be fascinated by an artist's rendering of Edgar Allan Poe's thirteen-year-old cousin.

"The board's decision was based on *your* recommendation," Ms. Langley hissed. "If you think this is going to happen quietly, you'd better think again."

Now it was the principal's turn to glance around before speaking. Peter flipped through another handful of pages in his book.

"We'll discuss this later—in a more appropriate setting," said the principal. Peter chanced another glance upward, just in time to see Mr. Steadham wheel the cart through the rear doors of the library. Ms. Langley sank into her desk chair, dazed and still shaking. She reached for her coffee mug and clasped it with both hands. She held it up but did not sip from it, and the steam from the liquid fogged her glasses. She yanked them off, tossing them to her desktop and rubbing her eyes.

24   Realizing that the bell would ring shortly, Peter remembered a science fiction novel he had wanted to read—*Stranger in a Strange Land,* by Robert A. Heinlein. He located it and brought it to Ms. Langley, who calmly scanned the book and handed it back to him. Her eyes, Peter thought, glistened as though wet.

"Get 'em while you can," she said quietly.

The bell rang, and Justin Ingler shot toward the door. It was amazing to Peter how slow that kid was during the class period and how fast he could move when it was over. Ingler flew past the magnetic security rails, and the tiny magnet in his backpack set off the alarm. Peter knew that the rails were designed to detect the thin metal strips in the binding of each library book, and he had guessed correctly that they couldn't tell the difference between the metal strips and a plain old copper-wound magnet.

Justin Ingler spread his arms and turned toward Ms. Langley. "What?" he said. "What'd I do?"

The librarian gazed at Peter and pursed her lips. She then turned to Ingler and made a "come here" gesture. Her other hand tapped the countertop. "Empty your backpack, Mr. Ingler," she said. "Right here." Every student but one paused to see what would happen next.

Peter gripped his book as he stepped through the door. He would have liked to have enjoyed Justin's suffering a moment or two, or perhaps daydreamed about Byte's plans, but all he could think about was Mr. Steadham, that stack of books, and the squeal of the cart's tires as they disappeared from the library.

2:55 P.M.

Eugenia "Byte" Salzmann stared at the classroom clock and willed the minute hand to move faster. As usual, her sixth period Survey of American History class sped by like freeway traffic, a dull blur of names, dates, and concepts, and today she was having trouble separating her Whigs from her Tories.

She smiled to herself. She had other things on her mind…

Her fingers tacked lightly across the keyboard of her laptop computer, which sat on the slanted desktop in front of her and annoyed her every few moments by trying to slide off into her lap. Worse, Mr. Lujan, the head of the history department at BPHS, had gone on one of his lecture binges, slapping down one transparency after another onto the overhead projector. Byte could hardly keep up.

She glanced up at the clock again: *2:58*

Byte clicked the Save icon and shut her computer down. In an eyeblink she had it zipped into its padded nylon case. Though Mr. Lujan was still rattling on about Thomas Paine and *Common Sense,* turning over transparencies with mind-numbing speed, Byte dumped her history book into her backpack. It now lay next to her trig book, her folded canvas lunch bag with its rainbow-colored Apple logo, and her Save the Rain Forest pencil case with the picture of a spider monkey on the front.

When the bell rang, she jumped to her feet, clutching the laptop case to her chest and swinging the pack across her shoulder. A loud *oof* burst from her when the heavy weight landed between her shoulder blades. Worse, all this sudden movement—the shifting of the heavy bags—made her lose her balance for a moment. Byte stood with her hand on her desk to steady herself, her long, skinny legs splayed out like a newborn colt's.

But she was out the door before the bell stopped ringing.

She stopped at her locker before pushing through the crowded hallway to the exit. Then… *free!* Her hand hit the steel crash bar and she thrust the door open, stepping out into blazing sunlight, catching the hint of salt in the air from the nearby beach. Like a music box tinkling off the last few notes of its song, Byte moved more and more slowly until she came to a stop in the middle of the steps. The air was cool, and a breeze tossed her brownish blond air in tangles across her face. The chatter of the students around her, the occasional laugh, faded into a background noise that was almost musical.

The rear of the school faced the student parking lot, four outdoor basketball courts, two tennis courts, and a quarter-mile oval running track. Byte walked toward the parking lot, her eyes peeled for a battered minivan.

"So," said a voice from behind her, "when do we dive for cover?"

Mattie. He appeared at her side as if from nowhere, and Byte threw an arm around his neck, hugging him to her and, for just a moment, choking him solidly.

"Okay, okay," he said laughing. "Lemme go and show it to me."

"That's better," said Byte.

She took Mattie by the hand, pulling him along behind her until they reached the edge of the basketball courts. Here they could sit down on one of the concrete benches, several of which were strewn with shirts discarded by members of the JV basketball team, who were playing pickup in the afternoon sun. Byte led Mattie to an empty bench, and the two sat. She grinned and tugged at the zippers of her computer bag.

Mattie put a hand on hers, stopping her from continuing. "Wait a sec," he told her. He pointed back at the rear steps of the school. "Look."

Jake and Peter were walking toward them.

"They'll want to see, too."

Jake strode toward Byte and Mattie with his shoulders back and his clarinet case dangling from one arm. Byte noticed he was wearing his band jacket with its leather sleeves and BPHS Tigers logo. As he approached, she could hear the jacket jingling with the dozen or so award medals pinned to the front.

"So you're finally legal," said Peter. "Congratulations."

"Hmmm?" said Byte, still looking at Jake. "Oh, yeah! Come look."

She unzipped the outer section of her computer case and laid it open like a book. Jake looked down from over her shoulder, and Peter knelt in front of her to see better through his thick glasses.

28   The case contained loops for pens and pencils, slots for credit cards, and two window pockets. In the left window was Byte's Bugle Point High School student ID, with its cardinal and gold trim. Byte's gold-rimmed granny glasses had a habit of slipping to the tip of her nose, and she would often crinkle her nose to push them back up. The school photographer had shot the photo without warning, and he had caught her at just that moment. She had stared straight at the camera, the bright studio lights casting a yellow tint over her pale skin and, worst of all, one eye half-shut and her nose wrinkled up like a baby pig's snout.

Byte quickly slammed her palm down over that one.

In the right window, though, was another photo ID, this one bearing the official seal of the state of California. In tiny print it listed Byte's name and address, her date of birth, her social security number, and, in proud letters, the words Class D. The photo, though looking like something one might see on a missing child notice at the post office, was still a striking improvement over her school picture. Byte's face stared up from the license with a giddy smile and a flash of glare off the lenses of her glasses.

"Nice picture," said Jake.

"Awesome," added Peter.

Mattie stared at the license and frowned. "Boy, they'll give one of these to just anybody, won't they?" he said. Byte swatted his shoulder with her hand.

As she zipped the compartment closed, she heard laughter from the basketball court behind her. Byte turned in time to see a basketball hurtling toward her. It struck the ground a few feet in front of her and bounced upward, knocking the computer off her lap. The computer landed on the blacktop and skittered several feet before coming to a stop.

My computer! Byte lunged for the case and turned it over, checking it for damage. The case was made of heavy-duty Nylon. Byte brushed at the dirt and scratches on the bottom of it, licking her finger and rubbing at the worst spots. Then she closed her eyes and took in a deep, calming breath. *It'll be all right,* she thought. The dense padding likely protected the laptop, but she would plug it in and check it—once she was far away from the basketball courts.

"*Ooooooppps,*" said a voice.

Byte clutched the case to her chest and spun in the direction of the voice. Toby Atherton, the center on the JV basketball team, stood at the edge of the court, his arms folded and a suggestion of a smile on his face. His thin hair hung down his forehead, plastered with sweat. "My bad," he said. He looked over his shoulder at his friends on the basketball court, giggling stupidly, but they didn't react. A couple gazed at him like statues. One ran to get the basketball, shaking his head as he did, and another just stared at the ground, scuffing his toe against the black tar.

"Your *bad?*" said Byte. She stood up taller, straightening her skirt. Her glasses had gone askew when the ball hit her, and she grew more frustrated as she tried to adjust them. She finally yanked the glasses off and thrust them to Jake, who was standing behind her. He took them, but his other hand came down on her shoulder, squeezing it to calm her.

"Easy, girl," he whispered.

Byte shrugged his hand off and continued talking to Toby Atherton, who stood there with an idiotic grin on his face. Byte's anger flamed inside her. She heard her voice begin at a level tone and listened as it climbed to a shout. "You knock a twenty-two-hundred-dollar computer off my lap, and all you can say is that it's your *bad*? Is that some kind of non-apology used by brainless… *donkeys*…who are too egotistical to admit it when they've done something *really stupid*?"

Atherton glanced at Peter, Jake, and Mattie, measuring them, then took a few steps forward. Though Jake was more muscular than the basketball player, Byte noted that Atherton was taller, and his large hands were thick and bony. His smile faded as he approached the group, flattening into a smirk as his eyes centered like lasers on Byte. "Well," he said, "if it isn't the computer chick." Once again he looked over his shoulder at his friends, calling to them. "Hey look, guys, it's the computer chick."

One of them—the one who had been scuffing his toe against the blacktop—said, "Knock it off, Toby."

Byte felt a prickling at the back of her neck. Atherton's smug mouth and arrogant eyes made it obvious. The basketball slamming into her computer was no accident.

Jake silently stepped around Byte, interposing himself between her and the basketball player. Peter and Mattie moved forward too, and Byte suddenly felt her alarms clanging. *No*, she told herself. This would not turn into a fistfight. She'd let Atherton know exactly what she thought of him, and if the computer was broken, she'd make it clear he would pay for it.

Just then a horrible squealing sound came from behind Byte, a shriek of metal grinding against metal. She turned to see a teal green minivan pull to a stop just a few feet away. The stereo system inside the van blared a Led Zeppelin song, which cut off in midchorus when the driver shut down the engine. The van rocked a bit, still struggling with the sudden command to stop, then came to a rest.

The door opened, and a tall man stepped out. His hair was thinning on top, but the back was long and drawn into a ponytail. He wore scuffed cowboy boots, a plaid flannel shirt, and faded jeans with shredded cuffs and a large hole in the right knee. A bushy mustache curled over his upper lip and down past the corners of his mouth. Two or three days' beard growth darkened his face and chin.

"Uncle Joshua!" Byte cried.

She ran over to him and threw her arms around his neck. As she did, the tension she had been feeling drained out of her. No fight would break out now. An adult had walked onto the scene, and, even better, the adult was Uncle Josh.

"Hey," he said, "you ready?"

He was speaking to Byte, but she noticed that his eyes were looking past her—at her friends, at Toby Atherton's smoldering expression. The corners of his eyes crinkled, like he was remembering a joke, and he smiled warmly. However, Byte studied his expression a moment longer and noticed that behind the smile he seemed to be measuring the situation.

He knows we were arguing.

"So," said Joshua, walking over to the boys. The smile never left his face. "What's the problem here?"

"No problem," said Atherton.

Peter, Jake, and Mattie stood silent.

"*Really,*" said Josh. He looked around at the basketball court and drew in a deep breath, as though a certain "basketball smell" hung in the air and he wanted to take it in. "You know," he said, "when I was in high school, we didn't fight much. If we had a problem with somebody, we'd go out to the basketball court and settle it with a little one-on-one."

At this, Byte covered her face with her hands. *Oh, no...*

"So, what do you say?" Josh went on. Apparently he had already figured out who the problem was. Byte peeked between her fingers and saw that Uncle Josh was staring directly at Toby Atherton.

Atherton snorted. "Against *you*, old man?"

Josh spread his arms. "Why not? First to reach ten points is the winner."

At this Atherton laughed. He looked at the boy holding the basketball and gestured for it. The boy bounced a pass to him and Atherton, without warning, caught the ball, spun, and fired a blistering pass at Josh's midsection. Josh caught it easily, the ball slapping sharply against his palms.

"Let's understand some rules before we start," Josh went on. "First—because I am the old man here, and of course in danger of keeling over from a heart attack at any moment, I get the ball first." And now Josh's eyes positively gleamed. "And…we play winner's outs."

"What's winner's outs?" whispered Mattie.

"In regular basketball," Jake whispered back, "when you make a basket, the other team gets possession of the ball. In winner's outs, you get to hold on to the ball when you score."

Peter looked aghast. "And he *wants* that?"

Byte smiled at her friends and said nothing. She merely gestured for them to step away from the court.

Josh set down the ball to tug off his shirt and toss it to Byte. He then yanked out the tail of his T-shirt and took a position at the top of the key. He flipped the ball to Atherton, a signal that he was ready to begin play, and Atherton once again looked at his friends. He grinned broadly, already certain of his victory. When none of his friends grinned back, the smile vanished from his face, and he tossed the ball back to Josh.

The game had begun.

Josh faked left, moved right, and jumped. Atherton never made it back from the fake. The ball left Josh's palm in a high arc, floated for a moment, then dropped through the net with a gentle *thwish*. Atherton caught the ball and fired it back to Josh, moving in now to guard him a little more closely.

Josh drove inside. Atherton was easily quick enough to keep up with him, so Josh pulled up, dropping back into a fadeaway jump shot that sailed over Atherton's flailing arms. It banked gently off the backboard and fell through the hoop, bouncing several times before rolling up to the high-schooler's ankles. Atherton just stared at him, his jaw hanging and his chest heaving for air.

Mattie set his hand against his cheek as though he were holding a phone. "Hello?" he said, "911?"

The rest of the game played out much the same way. Josh was shorter than Atherton, and didn't seem to move anywhere near as quickly, but he always seemed to be someplace Atherton wasn't. Atherton leaped high to grab rebounds, making a big show of jamming his elbows back and forth as he came down with the ball. Josh, in contrast, just seemed to know where the ball was going to be and always happened to be there waiting for it. While Atherton dribbled all over the court, wearing himself out, Josh never held onto the ball very long. One or two dribbles, a fake, and *swish*.

And with every shot Josh made, Atherton had to give the ball back to him.

"Eight to four," Josh said. "Game point."

Atherton staggered up once again to guard him, his T-shirt drenched and clinging to his skin, his hair a wet mop. He bent over, his arms braced against his knees as he sucked in one breath after another.

Josh didn't even dribble the ball. He smiled at Atherton, dipped his knees, and jumped. The ball sailed over Atherton's head and whisked through the net.

At this, the game-winning basket, Toby Atherton's arms hung like wet spaghetti at his sides. Josh reached down for the teen's right hand, gripped it in a handshake, then let it drop again. "Good game," he said.

Atherton blinked at the words, unable to speak.

Josh walked back to the bench. He stripped off his sweaty T-shirt, wiped himself down with it, then reached for his flannel shirt and put it back on. When he finished buttoning the shirt, he sat down on the bench and pulled up the leg of his jeans.

Toby Atherton gaped.

From just below the knee, Josh's left leg was a custom-fitted artificial limb. Josh loosened the straps that held the prosthesis in place and slipped it off, revealing a bandaged stump. He massaged the stump with his hand and grinned at Toby Atherton. "Kinda chafes a little when I play basketball, you know?"

"Yeah...sure," said Atherton—as though, yes, he understood perfectly well how uncomfortable it was when one's artificial limb chafed.

Josh slipped the limb back on, secured it, and stood, testing his weight and balance against it. When he was satisfied, he looked at Byte. "Ready?" he asked.

"Ready," she said. She gathered up her backpack and computer bag. Josh tossed the car keys to her, and she snatched them from the air with one hand.

Josh nodded at Peter, Jake, and Mattie. "Your friends coming with us?"

"Nah," said Byte. "They'll be joining us later." She looked at the three, and for the first time since the basketball game had started, she noticed the expressions on their faces. All seemed as shocked as Toby Atherton was.

36   "You know," said Mattie, "speaking as the shortest person here, I'm *really* glad I got to see this."

Byte tossed her bags in through the van's side door, slammed the door shut, then climbed into the driver's seat. Uncle Josh slipped into the passenger seat next to her.

"Here goes," Byte said.

Taking a deep breath, she slid the key into the ignition and felt the van's engine rumble to a start. She then put the car in gear and slowly wheeled it into a turn. As she pulled out of the parking lot, she couldn't resist a final look at the basketball court. Peter and Jake waved to her. Mattie circled his arms around his head and crouched to the ground, feigning a duck-and-cover drill as the mini-van crept past.

Toby Atherton sat alone. His friends had wandered off, and now he rested beneath the basketball goal, his back against the steel post, his eyes following the retreating van. The basketball lay on the ground between his knees.

"You know," said Byte, easing the van from the parking lot, "that guy's never going to forget what happened today."

Josh shrugged. "Good. That boy needed his butt whipped."

chapter two

Tuesday, 6:00 P.M.
Maggio's Italian Restaurant

You should order the calzone," said Mattie. Byte didn't bother to look up from her own menu. "I know what I want, thanks."

"Okayyyy," said Mattie, "but you'll like the calzone better. Trust me, I'm Italian."

Though it was a weeknight, Maggio's was packed, the room abuzz with voices and the clinking of glasses and silverware. The group sat at a huge round table draped in a red-and-white checked tablecloth. While Peter, Jake, Mattie, and Byte chattered about the menu, Byte's mom and Uncle Josh discussed the wine list. Jake reached into the woven basket in the center of the table and snatched a bread stick that glistened with garlic butter. The dinner had been Uncle Josh's idea, a party to celebrate Byte's getting her driver's license.

"I'm gonna have the chicken cacciatore," said Jake.

Mattie sighed and shook his head. "You'd like the linguine better."

38   Peter was staring at his menu, but Byte had the distinct impression he was looking at it without really seeing it. A thick lock of hair—the one that was always falling across Peter's eyes—slipped down now, but he didn't bother to brush it aside.

"Peter?" asked Byte. "Something on your mind?"

"Hmm?" he said. "Oh…not really."

Byte continued to look at him over her menu, not entirely satisfied with his answer.

He nodded—*I'm fine*—but the muscles in his jaw tightened, and tiny wrinkles cut across his forehead. "Something happened today in the library. I'll tell you later."

The waitress arrived, dressed in an ankle-length, multicolored skirt and a top with poofy sleeves and an elastic neckline. Like the other waitresses, she had tugged the neckline down across her shoulders, presumably because it made her look like a peasant girl from the Italian countryside. Byte thought the plastic name tag and the large button proclaiming Try Our Sicilian Scampi! sort of spoiled the illusion.

"Hi, my name is Celia. I'll be your server tonight. Are you ready to order?" She had long brown hair and olive skin. With a quick gesture, she swept an order pad and tiny pen into her hands and stood poised to write down the order.

Uncle Josh set down his menu and glanced at the others. "Everyone ready? Yes?" To the waitress he said, "We'll have a Caesar salad to go around." He pointed to the waitress's button. "We'll definitely want to start with a couple of orders of those Sicilian scampi, and I will have the mostacciolli. How about you, Donna?"

"I think I'll have the same," said Byte's mom.

"Fettuccini for me," said Byte. "If the sauce is vegetarian."

The waitress nodded. "It can be."

Jake frowned, cleared his throat, then raised his index finger and pointed down at the menu. "I'll have this," he said. The waitress glanced over his shoulder and nodded, scribbling the item onto her pad.

"Can I have the calzone?" asked Mattie, emphasizing the word and eyeing Byte as he spoke.

"Honey," said the waitress, grinning, "with a face like yours, you can have whatever you want."

Mattie beamed at the others. Byte's mother, who was almost a dead ringer for Byte with her curly hair and sharp nose, reached over and lightly pinched Mattie's cheek between thumb and forefinger, jiggling the skin.

A moment later the restaurant door swung open. While the group continued to order, Byte watched a man enter carrying a battered guitar case in one hand and a small amplifier in the other. A fabric duffel bag lay slung across his shoulder. Grimacing under the heavy load, he made his way to a carpeted platform that supported a plain wooden stool and an empty microphone stand.

"Hey," said Mattie, tugging at his sleeves, "when the food comes, betcha I can make a meatball disappear right before your eyes."

Donna Salzmann reached over and touched Mattie's arm. "Remember the taco incident?" she warned.

40   Mattie's mouth formed the word "oops" without saying it aloud. "Oh, yeah," he said. "Right. Bad idea."

The singer set up quickly, adjusting the microphone, plugging in the amp, and tuning his guitar. He leaned into the mike a couple of times saying, "Check…check," then went back to the amp to twist the knobs some more.

Uncle Josh raised his water glass. "I just want to remind everybody," he said, "that we are here to toast Byte's achievement. She has reached the summit. She has attained the ultimate symbol of teen freedom. She has— drum roll please—*earned her driver's license!*"

Byte felt Jake's hand touch her shoulder as he leaned over and whispered to her. "Is that why we're here?" he asked. His breath tickled her ear as he spoke, and Byte felt her face warming. "I thought we were celebrating the fact that you two survived the trip home."

Byte laughed and swatted him with her napkin.

A few moments later the waitress returned with a tray filled with salad and scampi appetizers and began serving the table.

The singer introduced himself as Red Carlyle, his voice whispery and his eyes cast down toward the floor.

While Byte and her friends chatted, he strummed a couple of chords, then sang a long series of old-time folk songs. The singer's voice was a reedy tenor, and Byte decided after she heard several songs that she liked it. It seemed to suit the music he chose—songs about freight trains, dusty roads, lost love, and men who were "hobos," back in the days before someone decided to call them "homeless" instead.

Byte finished her meal slowly, her attention drawn to the man onstage. She noticed that the singer had distracted Uncle Josh as well. Josh had served himself huge amounts of food, talking and joking all the while, but every now and then he glanced over at the stage with a faraway look in his eyes. The singer sang "Suzanne" and "If I Were a Carpenter," songs Byte's mother used to sing when Byte was a little girl. Josh cocked his head toward the stage and closed his eyes, as though trying to hear something other than the words and music.

"Oh, dear," said Byte's mom. "This sure brings back memories."

Uncle Josh said nothing. He just stared at the singer, his second helping of Sicilian scampi lying untouched.

The singer strapped a metal harness holding a harmonica around his neck. He sang "Blowin' in the Wind," wailing on his harmonica after each refrain.

Uncle Josh's wineglass slipped from his fingers and crashed to the floor.

"I'm sorry," he said. "I'm sorry." He bent down to pick up the broken pieces, but a busboy scooted over to sweep away the glass and wipe up the spilled wine. Josh apologized several more times, even after the busboy had hurried off.

Byte's mom leaned over. "Are you okay?"

His eyes locked on the singer. "It's him, Donna," he said. "It's *him*."

Byte looked over at her mom, and her mom shrugged.

Josh rose from his chair and walked toward the stage. He generally walked with a normal gait, though he had lost his leg below the knee. But now, Byte noticed, he dragged his false leg a bit as he made his way to the stage. The singer paused between songs and watched Josh approach.

Byte slid from her chair and followed her uncle. When she caught up with him, he was drawing a five-dollar bill from his wallet and dropping it into a glass fishbowl at the edge of the stage—the singer's tip jar. Byte noticed now that the man was wearing tattered jeans and a frayed University of Toronto sweatshirt. His hair was longish and carrot red—a little darker than the color of his beard and flecked here and there with gray. His eyes crinkled deeply at the corners, and the deep circles below them made him look both tired and sad.

"I'd like to make a request," Josh said flatly.

"Name it." The singer's reply was gruff, Byte thought, but the sadness in his face seemed to temper the gruffness.

"'Vietnam Rag,'" Josh said.

The singer turned away and reached for a bottle of water he'd left on top of his amp. When he turned back he eyed Josh, taking a deep swig of the water and wiping the back of his hand across his mouth. "Don't believe I know that one," he said.

"Sure you do," said Josh. "You know… 'say, Mr. President, la da da da da…'" Josh hummed a bit of the song, his voice catching after a line or so. Byte heard a tiny falsetto crack, and Josh swallowed and stopped humming.

The singer shook his head.

"Uncle Josh," said Byte, "he says he doesn't know it. Come on back to the table." She took his hand and started to draw him away, but Josh resisted. Byte tugged lightly on his arm, and he turned around to look at her. He blinked several times as though confused—as though he hadn't known she'd been standing next to him. "Are you all right?" she asked. He said nothing, just nodded and walked back to the table.

Byte hesitated. Instead of following her uncle, she reached down and took a business card from the stack sitting next to the fishbowl. The card bore a guitar logo surrounded by bold printing: Anthony "Red" Carlyle. Music. Lessons in Guitar, Bass, Banjo, Mandolin. An address and phone number appeared at the bottom. Byte carried the card with her to the table and set it down in front of Peter, who made a point of taking a business card from everybody. "Here," she said. "Been hanging around you too long, I guess."

Peter raised an eyebrow, glanced at the card, then slipped it into the pocket of his shirt.

As Byte and her uncle took their seats, the waitress returned to the table. She clapped her hands together. "Okay," she said, "shall I clear these away?"

Byte looked at her uncle, who remained silent, staring at the singer onstage like a man staring at the epitaph on his own gravestone.

Maybe Josh'll feel better once we get home, Byte thought.

Red Carlyle had taken a break right about the time the dessert tray arrived, stepping from the stage and vanishing. Uncle Josh took a fork and poked holes in his slice of cheesecake, eyeing the guitar and lone microphone stand.

Byte realized that her friends had not really noticed Josh's silence. Peter was trying to explain the difference between neutron stars and brown dwarf stars to Byte's mom, who nodded with feigned interest and threw a desperate rescue-me! look at Byte. Jake and Mattie had found room for two desserts each. Mattie wiped a napkin across the crumbs of cherry cheesecake around his mouth and swept his tongue along the sticky film that remained.

In the singer's absence, the restaurant switched to instrumental music, which felt flat and artificial in comparison to Red Carlyle's husky voice. The difference, Byte thought, was like looking at a photograph of a dog as opposed to having a real one jump up and lick your face.

The sun was beginning to set as they left the restaurant. Byte looked at her uncle, her hand extended. Josh took his keys from his pocket and glanced at Byte's mom. Mrs. Salzmann sighed and nodded, and Josh tossed the keys to Byte. She gripped them for a moment, then held them loosely, savoring the way they jingled as she walked. Byte and her mom took the front seats; Uncle Josh and the other Misfits piled in the back.

Mattie poked his head over Byte's shoulder as she fastened her seat belt. "Hey," he said. He pointed at Byte's clothes, then gestured behind him in the general direction of Uncle Josh. "Now I know where you get it."

Byte looked down at her clothing—at the tie-dyed T-shirt, the jeans with the wide, flaring bottoms and embroidered cuffs, the imitation leather jacket with the fringe across the chest, back, and sleeves. "Get what?" she asked.

"Your *sixties style*," Mattie said.

Jake grabbed Mattie by the back of his shirt and yanked him back into his seat.

"I was just making an observation," Mattie grumbled. "Some people inherit blue eyes or high cheekbones; others inherit…*hippie*."

Byte guided the van out of the parking lot and onto the thoroughfare. She had already made up her mind that she would follow the Old Shore Road instead of taking the interstate. The interstate was faster, a straight shot through Bugle Point with views of nothing but road signs, gas stations, and billboards calling out to weary drivers: McDonald's 1.5 Miles, Turn Left. Shore Road, however, lay along the coast, tracing the curves of the Pacific and sweeping up to the height of the cliffs that overlooked the Bugle Point marina. At night, from the highest of these cliffs, the lights of the marina looked like a field of stars someone had tossed at your feet.

46   When Byte pulled onto Old Shore Road, she saw her mom fold her arms tightly across her middle. Donna Salzmann threw a glance at Byte, then turned away quickly, a weak smile on her face.

"Mom, I can *handle* it," said Byte.

"She can handle it, Mrs. Salzmann," echoed Peter from the back.

"It's a breeze," chimed Jake.

Mattie stuck his head between the front seats again. "Would you let me out here?" he asked. Then: "*Oooooofff.*" Jake had yanked him back again.

Byte followed the road for twenty minutes, avoiding the frequent turnoffs that led toward the beach. She could feel the minivan chugging, working harder as it climbed the steep hills and the downtown dropped away below them. The old highway would continue to climb like this, twisting to follow the ragged cliff face, until the marina lay almost two hundred feet below.

As the minivan continued to climb, Byte tensed. To her right was the face of the cliff. To her left was a single lane of oncoming traffic. Beyond that was nothing but a guardrail and a very long drop to the marina below. Shrubs sprouted from the cliff face, casting odd shadows in the twilight. Once or twice Byte saw tiny pine trees growing out *sideways* from the cliff, their trunks bending upward to find the sun. Now, as she turned on her headlights, the image seemed almost surreal, and Byte thought that perhaps—just perhaps—she should have driven Shore Road in the daylight a few more times before she tackled it in the gray-blue light after sunset.

Behind her Jake was humming to himself. Peter and Mattie kept up a quiet but steady chatter, arguing over their weapons of choice if they were suddenly marooned on an alien planet. Peter opted for a phaser; Mattie insisted on a lightsaber.

At the top of the climb, Byte breathed more easily. She glanced at her mom and saw that she, too, seemed more relaxed now that the road was starting to widen and the uphill part of the trip was at its end.

The road dropped a bit now, conforming to the shape of the cliff face. The van shot forward faster than Byte expected, going straight instead of easing into the sharp curve ahead. Byte yanked at the steering wheel, and the van swerved toward the cliff wall for an instant, then swung away.

"Don't worry about us," called Mattie from the back. "We're fine. No injuries back here, no sir."

Byte laughed. "Sorry."

She let up on the accelerator, but the van continued to pick up speed. Forty-five miles per hour. Fifty. Byte gripped the wheel, forcing the van to follow the road the way you might "guide" a Great Dane that was hauling you along by its leash. Her mother reached for the overhead handle. "Honey," she said, "you're going too fast."

Byte knew her mother was right. She sensed that the car was moving a little faster than she could control it, that she might graze the cliff face, or sideswipe a car

48 barreling in from the opposite direction. Crinkling her nose to set her glasses straight, she lifted her foot off the gas and eased it down on the brake pedal.

Nothing happened.

She pressed harder, until the pedal lay flat against the floor, offering no resistance. The van grazed the cliff face, a shower of sparks spraying off the edge of the front bumper.

"Byte!" shouted her mom.

Byte felt a hard, cold ball in the center of her chest. The cold spread outward, tingling down her back and along her arms. Her eyes could only dart from one terrifying image to another: the narrow road, the dizzying drop to the marina, the cliff face, the speedometer needling upward. Josh was saying something, but Byte was too focused on the road to pay attention. Her voice came out in a whimper. "Mom?…"

"Brake, honey," her mom said. She was gripping the handle with both hands now.

"I'm *trying*," Byte shouted. "It's not working!"

Her friends' voices became louder and more animated, their words a helter-skelter mishmash that was no easier to follow than the road. Uncle Josh was shouting now, but Byte couldn't make out what he was saying—something about sparking?

Fifty-five. Sixty. The van plummeted down the hill.

Soon they would hit the outer edges of a residential area—cross streets, stop signs, kids playing. Ahead was Oceanview Park, where Byte saw half a dozen kids playing football under a streetlight.

"Byte!" shouted Uncle Josh. "The parking brake!"

Of course! In her fear, she had forgotten. She reached for the parking brake and yanked upward.

Screeeeeeeee…

The wheels locked, and the van fishtailed. Byte heard Mattie cry out, then felt a tremendous thump as the van hopped the curb and ran onto the grass. The kids yelled and scattered. Byte yanked at the steering wheel and found that, with the tires locked, it did no good. She stared in horrified fascination through the windshield at the trees ahead. Her mother screamed, a loud, throat-tearing sound that keened to a high pitch and stayed there. The van's tires carved deep ruts in the grass, and the trees—those trees that just kept leaping around like stiff, silly dancers—grew larger and larger.

She heard a sound like a shotgun blast, and the windshield shattered into a huge spiderweb. A great bolt of pain ran up her leg. She rocked forward toward the broken windshield, but the shoulder harness grabbed her and slammed her back into her seat.

The van teetered over on its side, and Byte's head slammed against the window.

eter felt cold glass on his cheek. He lay on his side, his shoulder cramped against the side of the van. Through the window below him, he could see grass, flattened and splayed where the glass pressed against it. His forehead hurt, and something wet trickled down from it across his cheekbone and along his chin.

A tremendous weight lay on top of him. Peter shifted, and the weight groaned. It was Jake. The larger boy moved, and Peter found he could breathe more easily. A whirl of motion then came from above Peter. He looked for Mattie and saw that the youngest Misfit dangled, uninjured, from his seat belt and shoulder restraint.

Peter could hear Byte sobbing quietly.

"Is everyone okay?" asked Josh.

No one answered right away. Peter examined his own injuries—the bruised ribs, the jammed finger on his left hand, the thick lump on his forehead. He brushed his fingers against the stickiness on his cheek and felt a trail of blood. No pain in his neck or back. No dizziness. He'd be fine.

Josh reached up and tugged on the door of the van and it slid open with a metallic squeal. Staring up through the opening, Peter saw the branches of a tree and a hint of stars staring down from a dark sky.

"*Hellooooo*," said Mattie. "What do I have to do to get a little help here, huh?" Josh hoisted himself through the van's door then reached in and hauled Mattie out.

Jake followed, pulling himself up through the door and leaping to the ground without help. Peter climbed out next. He stared down through the doorway at Byte. While inside, his view of her had been blocked by the seat in front of him. Now he could see her clearly, and he understood why she was sobbing. The van had struck the tree so hard that the engine had punched through the firewall. Peter could see the steering wheel bent upward, the dashboard and pedals caved in, two or three inches of sheet metal, insulation, and even a glint of the engine itself—right there in the passenger compartment! The interior of the van had crumpled in against Byte's right leg. At least Mrs. Salzmann seemed, for the most part, unhurt.

Sirens wailed, growing louder and closer.

"Byte," called Josh. "Can you move?"

Byte shook her head.

"Okay," said Josh. "We'll let the rescue team handle it. Donna?"

Mrs. Salzmann looked up at him. "I'm fine," she said quietly. "I'll stay here with Byte."

52 A crowd had formed around the van. The kids with the football huddled about ten yards away, their eyes wide and gaping, afraid to come any closer. A man rushed toward the van from across the street, holding a cell phone to his ear as he ran. He slid the antenna down and jammed the phone into his pocket when he saw the emergency vehicles pull up.

Peter felt his ability to focus slipping away from him. He heard the voices of the emergency techs, the squawk of their radios, and the hushed conversation of the onlookers, but it all seemed so faint and distant, as though he were watching it on television rather than living it. Josh was talking to a policeman, but Peter could not make out what either man was saying. An emergency tech lifted Mrs. Salzmann from the van and set her on the grass; another tech lay a blanket across her shoulders. Peter felt cold. He wrapped his arms around himself and shivered, noting that Jake and Mattie were doing the same.

It's not that cold, he decided. *Must be shock.*

His mind leaped back into focus when he heard Byte's voice howling in pain. A few moments later the paramedics brought her out of the van on a stretcher.

Josh must have mentioned the problem with the brakes in his statement, because a police officer was examining the van's underbelly. He gently tugged at a hose. It pulled apart, severed in the middle. The officer yanked off his cap to reveal a few strands of hair that were gleaming with perspiration. He brushed at the sweat with a handkerchief, then stuffed the handkerchief back into his pocket.

"Musta caught a sharp rock or something," he said. He shook his head at the fickle nature of the universe and scribbled something onto his report sheet. He eyed Peter, Jake, and Mattie. "I'll need statements from you too."

Jake walked over to the van, his eyes fixed on the brake line. Peter watched him, then motioned to Mattie that they should follow. Jake held the hose in his fingers and studied it.

"What are you thinking?" asked Peter.

Jake frowned. "I'm not sure. Look at this hose." He moved aside a bit so Peter and Mattie could better see the severed end. "Look how clean the cut is. It's not torn or ragged. Could a rock do that?"

"Well…yeah, maybe it could," said Peter, but as soon as he spoke he knew how unlikely it was.

"Looks to me," said Jake, "like it might have been cut— maybe with a knife or a razor or something."

Mattie's jaw went slack. "Wait," he said, "you're saying you think someone *wanted* us to have an accident? Who? Atherton?"

Jake's shoulders heaved. "Dunno. But the brake fluid would have run out in just a few minutes or so."

"That means it didn't happen at school," Peter said.

"Yeah, if someone cut the line, he did it while we were at the restaurant," Jake agreed.

"Byte's uncle seemed to have something going on with that guitar player at the restaurant," suggested Mattie.

54 Peter's mind raced. "Did the guy ever leave the stage?"

"He took a break," Mattie offered. "Ten, maybe fifteen minutes, remember?"

Peter shook his head. It didn't make sense. "Ten minutes is long enough," he agreed, "but it's crazy. Josh made this guy so angry that he decided to cut our brakes? He just happened to know which car was ours? And he just happened to have a knife or a razor with him? And he was confident enough and gutsy enough and—and *angry* enough—to just slide underneath and cut our brake line? Is that what you're saying?"

"He could have asked someone about the car," suggested Mattie.

"We parked in the back of the restaurant," added Jake. "Not many witnesses."

Peter said nothing. He wasn't satisfied, not satisfied at all. His eyes turned toward Josh—a man he perhaps only thought he knew. He lowered his tone carefully before speaking. "Okay," he said, "okay, then. Later we'll have a talk with Josh."

The emergency room at Mercy General Hospital smelled of disinfectant laced with an overdose of sweetened lemon—like furniture polish or liquid dishwashing soap. Peter's nostrils tingled and he snorted, rubbing his finger underneath his nose to get rid of the feeling.

Fifteen minutes ago a doctor had joined Peter in one of the examining rooms. The doctor stood a little shorter than Peter, was roundish in build, and sported what seemed to be a permanent frown. He tugged on a pair of rubber gloves and soaked a cotton ball with anti-septic, which he then used to clean the cut in the center of the rather large lump on Peter's noggin. Next came a squirt of ointment, which made the lump tingle, grow cold, then turn completely numb.

"How's that stuff work?" Peter asked, reaching up to touch the numb spot.

The doctor pushed Peter's hand away and reached for the needle and sutures.

Now, three stitches later, Peter sat in the waiting room—the waiting-for-Byte room—holding a plastic baggie containing some kind of blue gel against his fore-head. The gel was ice cold, like the ointment, and made his lump hurt, but the nurse told him it would reduce the swelling and he should hold it there until she told him he could take it off. Even now she eyed him from behind her desk at the glass window, frowning as she scrubbed her hands with antibacterial cleanser.

Mattie sat next to Peter, silent. He took a quarter from his pocket and held it in his fingers. Next he made a fist with his other hand and tapped the quarter three times against the back of the fist. With the third tap, the quar-ter disappeared. Mattie then opened the fist to reveal the coin resting in his palm. He did this trick over and over again, and Peter realized his friend was only slightly aware he was doing it. Jake, Peter saw, sat a few feet away, his arms folded and his left wrist wrapped in an Ace bandage. He was moving the fingers of his left hand—no doubt testing them for pain and seeing how the injury might affect his clarinet playing. Josh sat across the room, his head hanging down and his elbows braced against his knees. His shirt was torn, and Peter could see welts and bruises on the man's chest that must have formed when Josh's body was hurled against the seat-belt restraint.

Peter rotated his left shoulder, wincing at his own bruises.

Byte and her mother were in another exam room. Mrs. Salzmann, like Peter, had received three stitches. Hers ran across the right cheekbone, where her face had struck the dashboard. Byte…well, Byte was taking a little longer, and Peter no longer felt like sitting around waiting for another vague update. He limped up to the glass window and rapped on it with a knuckle.

"*Excuse* me," he said, a little sharply. "I know I've already asked once, but I'd really like to know how my friend, Eugenia Salzmann, is doing."

The nurse looked up from her paperwork and stared at him. She was young—no more than twenty-five, Peter decided—and blessed with blond hair so thick it threatened to collapse out of the careful system of barrettes, bobby pins, and clips she used to clamp it in place beneath her pointed white cap. "Mr. Braddock," she said. Peter noted the hint of a smile on her face, but also the clear message of impatience in her eyes.

And she remembered his name. Not a good sign.

"By my count, this is the *third* time you've come up to this window to ask about Ms. Salzmann. I can only repeat what I've told you before: Your friend has a broken leg. They're putting her in a cast now. That's all I know. You'll learn more about her condition as soon as the doctor is through, and you will definitely learn it more quickly if you will just remain in your seat and allow us to do our jobs, okay?" She then jabbed an extremely sharp pencil in the direction of the chair Peter had vacated.

Peter sat.

"Whadja find out?" asked Jake.

"Same old same old. She won't tell me anything more," Peter muttered.

He gestured toward Josh. "Come on. Our folks will be here to pick us up in a few minutes. While we're waiting, it's a good time for us to find out what happened in the restaurant."

Josh leaned back against the wall, his jacket thrown loosely around him like a blanket. He stared up at the ceiling, seemingly unaware of anything around him. Peter, Jake, and Mattie walked the few steps across the room to join him.

"Byte should be out soon," said Peter. "They're putting a cast on her."

"Great," said Josh. "That's great."

Peter gestured for his friends to sit. "Josh," he said, "we have to ask you something. Can you tell us what happened tonight? I mean, with that guy, the singer? You were acting strangely. Do you know him?"

Josh's eyes flashed, then he shrugged. He spoke in a voice so quiet Peter could barely hear him. "I—I don't know. I think so."

"Who was he?" asked Jake.

"I think—" said Josh, "I think he's the man who took my leg from me."

Peter, Jake, and Mattie listened as Josh took them back in time thirty years, to that violent Saturday at Trenton State. Josh told them about the protest movement against the war and why the National Guard was on campus. He spoke of the singer, Dylan McConnell, who shook his head *no no no* when three jeeps exploded and who ran away like a coward.

"They told me later," said Josh, "that my leg was hit by little tiny pieces of a jeep's fuel tank. Can you imagine? Dozens of bits of metal, most of them no bigger than your fingernail, went into my leg. Little pieces of *nothing!* Specks... But there were so many, like little razor blades…the doctors couldn't fix me. They had to cut my leg off. Two days later, the following Monday, was the massacre."

The word made Peter shiver. "Massacre?" he asked.

Josh glared at him, only half-kiddingly. "Don't they teach you kids *anything*? Look it up. You'll find it."

"So," said Mattie, "you think the singer—this Dylan McConnell—set the bombs that blew up the jeeps?"

Peter shook his head. "No," he said. "It's more than that, isn't it? You think this guy at the restaurant tonight, this Red Carlyle, *is* Dylan McConnell."

Josh nodded. "I—I'm not a hundred percent sure, but it looked like him. Sounded…a little…like him. And the way he acted when I asked him about the song… McConnell's song.…"

Peter leaned in closer to Josh, and the other two Misfits understood that they should do the same. "Josh," he whispered, "if this guy *is* Dylan McConnell, and if he suspects that you recognized him, how bad would that be for him?"

Josh shrugged. "What do you mean?"

Peter hesitated. He looked at Jake and Mattie, who nodded—*go on*—confirming they wanted to travel this path. "What I'm asking is this," Peter said. "If you could identify Dylan McConnell, would he want you dead?"

Josh remained silent, recovering from the shock of the question. Then, as he mulled it over, he nodded almost imperceptibly. "Maybe."

"We're not so sure the brake failure was an accident," Mattie explained.

"The line was cut too cleanly," added Jake. "I suppose a sharp rock could have done it, but it doesn't seem very likely."

Josh stared off into space. A little huff of breath escaped his lips, something like a laugh. He said nothing. He just sat there, revealing nothing more.

A swinging door opened, and Byte came rolling through it in a wheelchair. Her right leg, imprisoned from hip to ankle in a plaster cast, stuck straight out on the chair's elevated leg rest. Her mother stood beside her, and a bony nurse with sunken cheeks laden with heavy makeup pushed her from behind.

"She's had some painkillers," said the nurse, "so she'll be a little out of it until morning, but she'll be fine. Tomorrow you can try her on a pair of crutches."

"Thank you. Thank you so much," said Mrs. Salzmann. She gave Byte's shoulders a little squeeze and then rolled the chair over to where the others were sitting.

"Hi, Byte," said Peter. "How are you feeling?"

"You all right?" asked Jake.

"Cool chair," said Mattie. "Can I sit in it?"

Byte smiled a dreamy smile at them, her eyes half-closed. "I'm fine," she said. "Fine fine fine."

"Well…um, good," said Peter. "That's good."

Byte then threw a heavy-lidded look in Jake's direction. "Hey—do you know how gorgeous you are? I mean, really. Let's be serious here."

Jake giggled nervously.

Peter felt his mouth hanging open.

Mrs. Salzmann rested against the wheelchair's thick plastic arm. She drew Byte's head against her and rocked her daughter quietly back and forth. "We're going to get you home and put you in bed," she told her, cooing as though to an infant.

Byte leaned against her mother, her eyes closed. "I want some ice cream," she said. "Anyone want some ice cream? I would just really like some ice cream. Or frozen yogurt. Y'like frozen yogurt? Chocolate and raspberry swirl, with li'l candy sprinkles…."

Her voice trailed off.

Peter sat back in his chair, his arms folded. "Hmph," he said. "I guess we'll fill her in tomorrow."

Peter's parents were the first to arrive. FBI agent Nick Braddock strode into the emergency room wearing a red pajama top tucked into a pair of black dress slacks. Peeking out from beneath the cuffs was a sliver of red pajama pants. Catherine Braddock tore in behind him, a long coat thrown over her ankle-length nightgown. She ran to Peter, took his face in her hands and examined his injuries—the lump and the stitches—from several different angles. When she began running her hands through his hair, asking him again and again if he was sure he was all right, Peter had to slip off his glasses before she accidentally knocked them to the floor.

Mattie's grandparents walked in a few moments later. Vincent Ramiro had apparently been puttering around the garage, for he arrived wearing denim overalls and a flannel shirt with the sleeves rolled to the elbows. Grease darkened his fingers. Mr. Ramiro sniffed the antiseptic air and self-consciously wiped his dirty hands against the overalls' bib. Mattie's grandmother was a thickly muscled woman who, Peter knew, grew up in Alabama and used to skip school on the first day of hunting season when she was a little girl. She swatted Mattie on the shoulder, smiled and winked at him, and said, "Sit up straight. You're not hurt."

Jake's parents said little when they finally arrived. They nodded to the other parents, signed the same medical insurance forms the others had signed, and hurried Jake to the car. Peter felt a twinge of pity for them. Seth Armstrong, Jake's dad, worked long hours in the printing business he owned. He was successful, as far as Peter could deduce from Jake, but both he and Mrs. Armstrong seemed to have grown older from the effort—their faces lined and their hair recently tinged with gray.

Catherine Braddock looked at Mrs. Salzmann. "Donna?" she asked, "do you and Byte need a ride home?"

"Thanks, Catherine," Byte's mom replied, "but I've already arranged for a cab." Mrs. Salzmann glanced down at Byte, then at Josh. She drew in a deep breath and looked once more at Peter's mom, a smile of relief playing across her face. "We're fine," she said.

Peter said little on the way home. His parents, however, chatted in a way that, for them, verged on giddiness. Peter figured they were not only relieved that their son was all right but also exhausted at the end of a very long day. They laughed about the time Peter was three years old and had tried to join the cast of Disney's *Peter Pan*—by running full tilt into the glass of the television set. Peter's mom flipped the radio dial to an oldies station, and she and his dad argued cheerily over whether Elvis or the Beatles were the true kings of rock 'n' roll. Nick Braddock even did an Elvis impersonation, snarling out a bar or two of "Hunka Hunka Burnin' Love," leaving Peter to wonder briefly if his father's body had just been inhabited by aliens.

The evening grew quieter when they arrived home. Peter's mom, after checking his bandage for the third time, slipped into bed to watch the news on their tiny bedroom TV. Nick Braddock peeled off his coat, hung it in the closet, and moved to his study to finish up some computer work.

Peter crashed on the couch, one leg dangling to the floor and his arms splayed out over his head. He lay there for several minutes, his eyes refusing to close. *Now,* he thought, *might actually be a good time to do a little checking around about this Red Carlyle.*

He hauled himself from the couch and shuffled to his father's study. Nick Braddock sat at his desk, clearly in the middle of one of the countless reports he had to file as an FBI agent.

"Hey, Dad," said Peter, "can I ask you a favor?"

His father's eyes never left the computer screen. "Sure."

"If I give you a couple of names, can you see if there's an FBI file on either of them?"

Nick Braddock's fingers paused above the keyboard for a moment. He swung his chair around slowly and eyed his son. "And this would be about?…" he asked.

That question posed a bit of a problem. Peter did not really want to reveal what the Misfits were thinking about the severed brake line—mostly because he was not sure he believed it himself. Still, to get what he wanted, he knew he would have to say something. "Um…the singer we saw at the restaurant tonight. I just want to know if he's connected with—with another singer I've heard about."

Peter waited for the answer: *You know you'll have to explain this, son.* FBI files, Peter knew, were not exactly casual reading material for high school students. Yet Peter also knew that his father respected the little bit of detective work Peter and his friends had done in the past. He might bend the rules this one time—if only to satisfy his own curiosity. The question was this: just how badly did Nick Braddock want to know what Peter was getting himself into?

The FBI agent waited a very long time before answering. "What are the names?" he asked.

Peter grinned and stepped over to his father, gazing at the computer screen over Nick Braddock's shoulder. His father saved his work, went online, and accessed the FBI's secure website. After keying in the appropriate password, he was in. Peter stared at a large Federal Bureau of Investigation logo and several site buttons. When his father clicked on one, a screen appeared bearing a search bar.

Peter's father said, "Okay, ready."

Peter reached into his pocket for the business card Byte had given him in the restaurant. "Anthony Carlyle. AKA 'Red.'"

His father typed in the name, and after several moments of searching the computer beeped.

0 matches found.
"Not on file," Nick announced. "Must be one of the good guys. Who's next?"

"Try 'Dylan McConnell,'" said Peter.

Mr. Braddock typed in the name. Again the computer whirred. This time, however, the blue bar indicating a file was downloading stopped in midsearch. A window popped up asking the user to type in his/her name, the name of the FBI office requesting the information, and the agent's identification number.

Nick Braddock frowned at the screen. "Hmph. Never seen this before."

"What happened?" Peter asked.

"I don't know. I typed in the name you gave me, and some new security system came slamming down. Hang on."

He typed in the information, and the system once again asked him for his password. Nick shook his head and entered that information as well. The blue bar started moving again...**72%, 86%, 97%**...and a moment later the computer beeped a second time.

Your request will be processed within 24 hours.

"They'll locate the file tomorrow," Nick explained, "scan everything in it, and send it to me as an e-mail attachment."

"To this computer?" Peter asked.

Nick laughed. "You wish. No, to the secure one in my office. I'll let you know if I find out anything. In the meantime, we both need to get some sleep."

66   Peter nodded. No doubt it was the excitement of the day, the adrenaline rush during the accident, and the worry over Byte, but he hadn't felt the least bit tired all evening. Now though, at the mere mention of the word "sleep," what little energy he had drained from his body. His neck and knee were sore, the lump on his head throbbed, and his shoulder burned where he had slammed into the belt restraint. He mumbled his thanks to his father and turned toward the stairway that would take him to his bedroom.

    As tired and achy as he was, he couldn't fall asleep. Instead, he lay awake, staring at the ceiling, struggling to form a plan. Byte would undoubtedly miss school tomorrow, but the when she returned, the Misfits had much to do. They would have classes to attend, homework to catch up on, and sometime in between it all they would have to figure out if someone had tried to kill them tonight.

chapter four

Thursday
Bugle Point High School Library

Peter felt his face breaking into a grin as he stepped through the library doors. It was a stupid grin, he could tell, the kind that got away from you so that you'd almost want to reach up with your hands and pull the corners of your mouth down a little bit so people wouldn't stare at you and wonder where your mind had gone.

But Peter didn't care. And so what if he was missing lunch?

At a study table in the far corner of the library, dressed in a peach-colored granny dress with a white lace collar, sat Byte. She hadn't tied her hair in the ponytail Peter was so accustomed to seeing. Instead it fell in snarly curls that framed her face and tumbled down her neck and back. A pair of aluminum crutches leaned against a chair next to her. Her left leg, Peter noticed, bent demurely beneath the table, while her right leg, encased in plaster, stuck out in the aisle like a giant white log. She returned the smile and waved at him.

68 Mattie sat on the carpet next to her, scribbling on her cast with a red Marks-A-Lot. Jake sat with her at the table. He flipped, panic-stricken, through the pages of one of his textbooks, which meant he was positive he had completed a certain homework assignment but for the life of him couldn't find it.

As Peter approached, he saw what Mattie was scribbling on Byte's cast. It was caricatures of the Misfits, all four of them set down in simple lines and broad strokes. Peter angled his head to get a better view of his own likeness. The younger Misfit's hand darted against the plaster like a bug stinging, then retreating, then stinging again. Peter saw a triangle forming a narrow face, two huge circles for the owl-like frames of his glasses, a flat line to indicate a mouth—*no smile,* Peter noted—and squiggly frown lines on his forehead to show he was thinking.

"I don't look like that," Peter said, feeling his forehead wrinkle even as he spoke.

A loud *pop* sounded as Mattie re-capped the marker. He looked up at Peter and grinned. "Yeah, right."

"I've been doing my homework," Byte chirped. Her laptop lay open on the table in front of her, and as Peter and Mattie took their seats, she spun it around so they could see the image on the monitor. Large black letters against a red background said Trenton State: The Truth about April 13, 1970.

"The guy who set up this website is one of the survivors of the massacre."

Peter yanked a chair over and straddled it. In the hospital, Josh had seemed distracted in his description of that day, incomplete and vague in the details. Peter definitely wanted to hear this part.

"Don't ask me yet," she said, "I'm still doing the research. But trust me, you're not going to believe it." She clicked on one of the buttons, and the page resolved into a series of photographs. Byte scrolled down until she came to a shot of a young man in a National Guard dress uniform. His uniform cap sat tucked against his ribs, held there by his elbow as he stood at attention. He had shiny black hair that, though clipped short, still held a hint of a wave.

Byte's fingernail ticked against the screen as she pointed at the photo's caption. "His name is Angelo Guiseppe Donatto. He was one of the Guardsmen on duty when the jeeps exploded and Uncle Josh lost his leg." She looked at the boys. "I can get other names," she offered, "but this guy lives only about an hour away from here." She flipped open a spiral notebook, turned to a page, and slid the book across the table to Peter. On it was written Mr. Donatto's name and address.

Peter decided at that moment he was in love with Byte. "How'd you find out where he lives?" he asked.

The smile that spread across Byte's face was one of almost evil satisfaction. "Oh," she said, waggling her fingers over her keyboard, "I can find *anybody*."

Jake's eyes widened. "I don't ever want to get on your bad side," he said.

"Okay then," said Peter. "Two of us will have a talk with Mr. Donatto."

He then reached into his shirt pocket for Red Carlyle's business card and set it on the table next to the notepad. This next part would not be easy, he knew, but it was necessary if the Misfits were going to figure all this out. "There's something else," he said. "One of us needs to, well, go undercover and take guitar lessons from this Red Carlyle."

Mattie picked up the business card and studied it. "So we're gonna do…what?" he asked. "Torture him with bad guitar playing until he confesses?"

Peter sighed. "No. If we can get into his own space—his home, his studio, something like that—he might feel safe and let something slip."

Byte shrugged. "I'll do it."

"You can't do it," said Jake. "You're in a cast."

"What's that got to do with anything?" she snapped.

Peter held up his hands, palms out. "Byte can't do it," he said plainly, "because the guy has *seen* her. She walked right up to him in the restaurant, remember?"

"It should be me," said Jake. "At least I know something about music."

"Or I could do it," offered Peter.

"Oh, there's an idea," grumbled Byte. "Peter the wannabe rock star. That's believable."

Mattie listened as his friends argued. All three were talking at once now, their loud whispers overlapping until the words became little more than a hum. Ms. Langley, Mattie noticed, was watching them from her desk at the checkout counter. Mattie's eyes darted from one member of the group to another, and he meekly raised his hand. "It should be me," he said.

The others kept on talking as though they hadn't heard him.

"It should be *me*," he insisted in full voice, cringing when he caught Ms. Langley's glare. The others went silent and stared at him. "It should be me," he said again, "*okay?* I had my back to the guy at the restaurant. There's no chance he saw me. I could even, I don't know, cut my hair—maybe dye it or something. He'll never know."

Peter bent closer to Mattie and lowered his voice. "Okay," he said. "I just want you to know…it might be dangerous. It's possible this guy just tried to kill us. He may *already* be looking for another opportunity."

Mattie waved that idea away. "That's paranoid," he said. "The guy doesn't know who we are. He couldn't possibly find us."

As he spoke, his eyes happened to fall on Byte's computer and the image of Angelo Guiseppe Donatto. There the man was—located out of the past, with only a few keystrokes, by a teenager with a computer. No doubt Donatto, too, would have thought it impossible.

Mattie lifted a hand and stared at his fingers. "Maybe my fingers are too small for guitar," he said. "You think they're too small?…"

In a few moments the bell would ring ending the lunch period. Peter watched as Byte closed down her computer and Jake, having found his assignment, stuffed his literature book into his already swollen backpack. Mattie balanced a playing card on the tip of his nose, until Byte snatched it away to reveal that it had a wad of chewing gum stuck to the back.

Ms. Langley was still staring at the group. The hush-this-is-a-library look had left her face—replaced, Peter thought, with something else: Doubt? Confusion? Indecision? She slipped her glasses off and squeezed her eyes shut, pressing a tissue against her face. A moment later she rose and began walking toward the table where they sat. Peter's inner alarms rang. Ms. Langley always moved with speed and purpose—pounding the stapler with her fist, stacking books on the counter with a loud *thunk*, snatching the pencil from her hair to write a hall pass as though she were a doctor scribbling a prescription. Now she gave Byte's shoulders a squeeze before grabbing a chair from a nearby table and sliding it over to join them.

"I want to talk to you…" She looked at each of them in turn. "All of you, before you just happened to show up at school one day to see things had changed."

"Changed?" asked Byte. Ms. Langley's tone was quiet and serious; this was not the brash librarian they had come to know over the last three years. Peter watched as Byte's eyes flitted across Ms. Langley's face, searching for clues in her eyes and the corners of her mouth.

"Yes," said Ms. Langley. "I think you know—well, you all know you've been special to me, and I wanted to tell you about this myself before it happened." She focused her gaze now on Byte. "I'm resigning my position as librarian."

Byte's eyes widened. She recoiled, leaning back in her chair. "You're *leaving?*" she cried.

"I don't want to go into details," said Ms. Langley, "but Karen Riggins, the chancellor at the university, has been wanting me to join their library staff for a number of years now. I'm thinking I might take her up on the offer."

Peter stared at the librarian. "Is this because our new principal has decided to ban certain books from the library?" he asked.

Ms. Langley raised an eyebrow. "You know about that already, hmm?"

Peter nodded, then gasped as a spiral notebook slammed—*Whumph!*—against his chest. He raised his arms as a shield and peered between them at Byte. She was brandishing the notebook, ready to hit him again.

"You knew?" she cried. "You *knew* about this, and you didn't *tell* me?"

Peter cowered before her, his arms still raised. "We were *busy*, remember?"

Byte blinked several times, then set the notebook back down. She drew Peter to her in a hug, which made Peter wonder what other things he could do to make her mad.

"Sorry," she said, making a great show of folding her hands.

74 "S'awright." Peter turned once more to Ms. Langley. "I was pretending not to hear you the other day—you know, when Mr. Steadham came in. You were whispering, but I guess you both got a little angry and talked louder than you intended."

Ms. Langley nodded. She remained silent a few moments, slipping the pencil from her hair and twirling it in her fingers before putting it back. Peter understood. Talking to students about what went on between her and another staff member was not exactly professional behavior. Peter could see the librarian measuring what she could say, taking into account the fact that the Misfits already knew what the principal had done. "I've spent six years building up this library," she said. "I can't stop him from tearing it down, but I certainly won't sit by and watch while he does it."

Peter looked at her, studying the flash of regret that only momentarily crossed the librarian's face. "That was more than you meant to say, wasn't it?" he said.

"Yes," she replied, smiling, "but it felt good to say it out loud."

Byte leaned over, her injured leg sticking out even further into the aisle as she hugged the woman. Ms. Langley placed her hands against Byte's cheeks, her eyes brimming, then quickly rose from the table. Before leaving, she looked at each of them. "I'd better get back to work," she said. "Things to do. I'm ordering new books."

She forced a smile and turned back to her desk.

Byte watched her for a very long time. "We have to do something about this," she said flatly.

"We're sort of already working on a case," Mattie reminded her.

Byte leveled her gaze at him. "Now we're working on *two*."

Vietnam Veterans Memorial
National Mall, Washington, D.C.

It isn't true, as they say, that everyone weeps at the Wall.

Oh, many do weep. FBI Special Agent Paul Bonhoffer knew that much was true. He had come here enough times to know, to *see* it with his own eyes: Grown men collapsed on the ground before the Wall, their shoulders heaving. Many of them arrived in wheelchairs, or with limbs missing. Other times it was women in their mid-fifties carrying bundles of roses, women who'd become widows at an age when most had just graduated from college. They laid the flowers at the foot of the Wall, burst into tears, then walked away alone or stepped back into the arms of second husbands, who stood silent and uncomprehending.

Even now, after countless visits, Paul stiffened as he walked across the National Mall toward the Vietnam Veterans Memorial, gathering himself the way one might gather up the scattered pieces of a jigsaw puzzle.

No, not everyone wept. Paul would not. He stood straight, his shoulders back, his eyes focused on the huge flag that waved from atop the fifty-foot bronze staff marking the Memorial's entrance. The base of the staff bore the emblems of the five military services. Nearby, also at the entrance, was the cast bronze statue, *The Three Servicemen*, each of a different race, their faces full of doubt, and one in particular looking painfully young beneath a helmet that seemed much too large for him. From where they stood the three stared at the Wall, as though contemplating the names there.

I will not weep, Paul reminded himself. *I will not.*

The Wall itself lay in the shape of a giant V. One section pointed toward the Washington Monument, the other toward the Lincoln Memorial. Some seventy sheets of polished black granite formed the Wall. Paul could see reflected in its surface the grass, the nearby trees, portions of nearby monuments, even the dappled light from the reflecting pool.

He strode a hundred yards or so toward the apex, where the Wall was highest. From here it angled downward until, at its ends, it was only tall enough to accommodate one line's worth of names. Here, at the apex, the list of names was 137 lines tall.

Yes, the names.

Paul's eyes scanned over them, taking in as many as he could in a single, sweeping glance. Each person listed here, all 57,939, had gone off to the jungles of Vietnam and never returned. The artist who had designed the Memorial—Maya Lin, a young female college student struggling to finish her degree in architecture—had not listed the names alphabetically. Instead they appeared chronologically, in the order in which the men had died, listed year by endless year. Paul could start at the east side of the apex, in 1959, and walk until the wall came to an end. From there he could go to the west side and continue his walk, following it until he reached the apex again—where it listed those who had died in 1975. Paul always thought the arrangement a little odd, but fascinating. The war started and ended in the same place. Paul wasn't sure of the meaning. Was the artist saying that war was circular, that it never ended, it just started over again? Or that war itself had truly come to an end?

Either way, people who come here to seek out a loved one's name have to work a bit to find it. Which is good, Paul thought. *We should be willing to make a little effort to remember.*

Though he knew exactly where he was going, Paul chose to move slowly. He liked to look at the people who came to visit, to see the little pieces of the past they left behind. Most left flowers, of course, but many chose instead to leave a more personal memento. Here at the base of the wall was a framed medal, no doubt awarded for bravery to some veteran who had died in the line of duty. Over there was a great cluster of daisies, held down by a child's bronzed shoe. In another place Paul found a tube of red lipstick taped to a 45-rpm Beatles record. Lip prints of the same color marked the record where a woman had kissed it.

He made his way along the Wall, slowing as he approached the year 1973. He eyed the number at the base of one section of stone, and his eyes passed quickly over the next section, where the names bore markers at every tenth line to help visitors count.

There it was.

When he came upon the name, a chill went down his back and crawled out to the tips of his fingers. The letters sand-blasted into the granite were a little over half an inch high.

Hugh A. Bonhoffer.

Paul felt a faint quivering in his shoulders. He distracted himself from the feeling by standing straighter and by switching his briefcase from his right hand to his left.

Good morning, little brother.

Paul had taken a college deferment and gone to law school, missing the war. Hugh, a year younger than he, had been a skinny, slouching nineteen year old when he enlisted in 1965. Oh, Hugh was not a born patriot. He'd been stuck with a low number in the draft. Hugh had figured he'd be called up soon anyway, so he had quickly enlisted, figuring he'd at least get to choose his assignment.

But when Hugh stepped off the plane four years later, a group of antiwar protesters had seen him, muttering under their breath as he walked past them in his dress uniform with its single medal on the chest. One protester, a young man in a leather vest, walked up to Hugh and without a word spit on him. The saliva struck the medal and hung there until Hugh wiped it off with a handkerchief. Hugh lunged at the man and likely would have put him in a hospital if policemen at the airport hadn't broken up the fight. Funny, Paul thought, how the protester had been arrested and Hugh had been let go with a wink.

Something had clearly happened to Paul's skinny kid brother over those four years. Hugh came home a muscular man with a straight back, a firm handshake, and a way of making quick, confident decisions. His new maturity astounded Paul, who almost felt that *he* had somehow become the younger of the two. The airport protester had angered Hugh, grinding at his insides while he weighed job offers against going to college. Ultimately, he did neither. He prowled through the house, deep in thought. He closed the door of his room and played loud music until the walls vibrated. And after that day at Trenton State—that horrible, bloody day in 1970—Hugh signed up for another tour in Vietnam. Three years later—one month before he would have shipped home permanently—he stepped on a land mine outside of Da Nang and was killed.

Paul hoisted up his briefcase so that it sat wedged in his armpit, his fingers holding it at the bottom. Unlike Hugh, Paul *had* finished college. He had gotten his law degree.

And he had joined the FBI.

Inside Paul's briefcase was a thick file folder, one he had spent years compiling after the original investigation had faltered and languished. The name on the folder said Dylan McConnell. An agent in Bugle Point, a

80 Nicholas Braddock, had just yesterday requested information on that thirty-year-old case, tripping the additional security measures Paul had placed on the file.

So, Hugh, Paul thought, *this Braddock guy wants information. That means he has a lead.* Well, Paul Bonhoffer would follow that lead. And Dylan McConnell would burn in hell.

...And for you, Hugh, Paul added, reaching out to touch the name engraved in the stone, *my secret—our secret—will burn with him.*

W e don't have a guitar," Mattie's grandfather insisted.
"Yes, we do," said his grandmother.

"No, we don't."

"Yes, we *do*." Nadine Ramiro put down the chicken leg she had been nibbling, licked the grease off her finger-tips—*she'd slap my hand for doing that,* Mattie thought—then wiped them on a napkin. "We have my daddy's guitar, remember? It's packed away in the loft above the garage."

Mattie shrank a little on the inside. *Oh, that's bound to be a dandy one,* he mused.

He and his grandfather climbed into the loft after dinner and, sure enough, they found an old wooden guitar case, its surface covered with leather that had cracked and faded over the years. Under the glow of the loft's single, naked hundred-watt lightbulb, the case looked like the corpse of an alligator that had died and been left to rot in the sun. They hauled it down, Mattie blowing off great wads of dust and frequently stopping to wipe his filthy hands across the back pockets of his jeans.

When they got it into the house, Mattie took it into his room and shut the door behind him. He wiped the case down with a damp cloth and tugged at the rusty latches. They were stubborn. He had to use his Leatherman multi-tool to pry them up before they would move freely and allow the case to open. Mattie imagined he heard a little hiss of air, as though the case were a mummy's sarcophagus, opened after centuries of entombment.

The guitar was tiny, much smaller than he would have guessed from looking at the case. Its headstock was crown-shaped at the top, and it bore a gold Gibson logo, a decal that had chipped and flaked. The tuning keys were white plastic, the metal casing over their gears sprinkled with rust. He could not find any cracks in the wood, which gave him some hope, but the lacquer finish over the entire face of the guitar bore a weblike pattern of fine cracks. At the edges the instrument was a deep, rich black, but the color grew brighter around the soundhole, where it shone like an antique penny someone had polished.

He was surprised at how quickly his grandparents had said yes when he told them he wanted to take guitar lessons. He had asked them why they were so agreeable, and his grandfather admitted they were thrilled that he had asked for something other than an Amaze Your Friends at Parties! kit from the local magic shop, a nuclear device to disassemble in his bedroom, or something alive that had fewer—or more—than four legs.

Mattie ran his fingers over the strings. They were muddy looking, black with grime, and they made a sound like someone banging the lid of a trash can. No, worse—a trash can muffled in a blanket.

That's not good.

He walked over to his bedroom door, swung it open, and called out. "Hey, Grandma. Is there any way I can get a guitar that's maybe a little nicer than this one?"

"Sure, dear," she replied. "Get a job."

This one, he decided, would do.

He called the number on Red Carlyle's business card, and the same whispery voice he remembered from the restaurant answered the phone. Red Carlyle suggested Mattie could come by his home studio the day after tomorrow.

Saturday

Angelo Donatto's house lay on the cul-de-sac of a quiet suburban neighborhood filled with wood-frame and stucco houses. Jake's first impression was that all the houses looked exactly the same. Except for differences in color—a pastel pink one here, a pastel yellow one here—each one looked as if it had been built out of some kind of plastic model kit. Jake half-expected identical dads to step out the front doors, slip behind the wheels of identical sedans, and receive identical cheek-smack kisses from identical wives.

"That one?" asked Jake.

Peter pointed. "No. That one."

He parked his 1969 Volkswagen Beetle in front of a pale green house with a trimmed lawn accented by a brick flower bed. In the driveway sat a one-ton pickup truck, its flanks spattered with mud. Jake noted two stickers on the truck's bumper. One came from a Marine Corps recruitment office: The Few. The Proud. The other, once red but now faded by the sun to the color of a peach, said Keeping America Free—The NRA.

Jake's eyes widened. "Great. National Rifle Association," Peter said. "Let's talk nice. Our Mr. Donatto may be armed to the teeth."

A walkway divided the lawn in two and led to a concrete porch. Jake rang the doorbell and heard a clatter inside followed by the shuffling of feet.

Jake didn't know what he expected to see when the door opened, but it wasn't this. He stared into the face of a girl about his age. Her skin was pale and almost translucent, and he could make out a faint tracing of blue veins in her neck and along her shoulders, where her tank top didn't cover them. Her cheeks were sunken, and her eyes—very pretty eyes—were also shaded in blue, the color of a bruise.

And she was completely bald.

Jake swallowed.

"Can I help you?" she asked in a nasal voice—in a tone that, if Jake were inclined to be judgmental, he would have thought rude. It was *Can I help you?* combined with *You better not waste my time.*

Peter spoke up. "We'd like to speak to Angelo Donatto, if we could, please."

The girl swung the door wide with her foot. Without a word, she turned and retreated into the house. Jake and Peter took it as an invitation to follow.

"*Daaad*," the girl hollered. "There's someone here to see you!"

A voice from the backyard bellowed a reply. "Awright!" Jake heard what sounded like an old pushmower.

While they waited, the girl sat on a sofa that was white with a soft pink floral pattern. In front of the sofa was a cedar chest that served as a coffee table, and on top of the chest was a Styrofoam head model bearing a brunette wig with long, tumbling curls. The girl reached for a hairbrush and began styling the wig, though she seemed to brush it hard, almost tearing at it. She worked this way for a few moments, then eyed the boys.

"You *can* sit," she said.

Jake and Peter sat in two somewhat ratty, overstuffed chairs facing the sofa, and Jake surveyed the room. The television set in the corner aired one of those afternoon talk shows where hosts try their best to encourage fistfights between the participants. The furnishings in the room, he noticed, were old but serviceable, and showed little feminine touches here and there—a lace doily beneath a lamp, and on the mantel a tiny porcelain statue of a woman holding a cat.

And there were guns. Lots of guns.

Next to the living room was a small den. By leaning forward a little and peering through the doorway, Jake could see a wall-mounted display of firearms behind what was—he hoped—shatterproof Plexiglas and a locked door. Handguns. More than a dozen of them. Several appeared to be older, perhaps antique. Jake even recognized one he had seen in old war movies, a German Luger from World War II. Others looked new and quite…efficient. On another wall was a rack for hunting weapons. Jake saw two rifles and, judging by the pump handles and wider barrels, two shotguns. A line of trophies and medals sat on a shelf.

He looked at Peter, tilting his head toward the displays, and Peter nodded. He had already seen them.

The girl gave up on the wig and reached for an electric guitar that sat on a metal stand. It was deep red at the edges, lightening to a fireglow orange in the center. Jake recognized the guitar as a Rickenbacker, a less well-known make than some others but one that was finely crafted and expensive.

The girl clumsily tried to hammer out a rock lick, but her hand couldn't quite manage the stretch.

"Nice guitar," Jake offered.

"Yeah," said the girl, fingering the strings and not looking at him. "My dad buys me anything I want."

"The Beatles played Rickenbackers," Jake added.

The girl's eyes lit up, settling on Jake as though he had finally said something worthy of her attention. "*Yeah*," she said, her face breaking into a huge smile. "You like the Beatles?"

Jake smiled back.

At that moment a glass door at the back of the house slid open, and a man entered. He was stocky, with short curly hair that lay close to his scalp and a faint blue-black shadow on his face where he hadn't shaved. He rubbed his hands, which were heavily callused, before offering a handshake to the two boys. "I'm Angelo Donatto," he said. And then, with his daughter's bluntness, he added, "What do you want?"

Peter took control from here, which was just fine and dandy with Jake. He sat, watching the girl struggle again with the guitar. She glanced up at him, then her eyes darted back down to the instrument.

"Sir," said Peter, "we're, um, working on a project. You were one of the National Guardsmen at Trenton State in 1970."

Jake looked up. The man's expression hardened.

"And we were wondering if you could tell us anything about what happened on April 11. We especially want to know about the singer who was playing that day, Dylan McConnell. Do you know anything at all about him? Where he may have gone?"

Angelo Donatto shook his head. "No."

"Do you know a local singer," Peter went on, "a guy named Red Carlyle? We're wondering if maybe he and McConnell are the same person."

"No." He eyed the boys again, this time with even less warmth. "Anything else? I'm busy."

Peter waited a moment before answering, and Jake had a sense that he was weighing the advantages—and disadvantages—of pressing forward with more questions. He didn't take long to decide. The look on Donatto's face, the tension in his shoulders and arms, his curt answers—all of these suggested that Peter's light probing had already gone too deep.

"No," said Peter. "No, that was all." He reached into his wallet for one of the Misfits' business cards, scribbling his name and phone number on the back.

misfits inc.
investigations

Mysteries are no mystery to us!

Jake Armstrong
Peter Braddock

Matthew Ramiro
Byte Salzmann

"If you think of anything, please give us a call," Peter added.

Angelo Donatto stuffed the card in his shirt pocket without answering.

The girl walked them to the door. She opened it wide, guiding Peter out first but tapping Jake on the shoulder as he passed. "My name's Angela, by the way," she said. "My dad's Angelo—I'm Angela. Or Angie. My family's not big on imagination."

Jake stuck out his hand. "I'm Jake," he said. He was going to say more, but before he could, he noticed some movement at the front window. Mr. Donatto stood there, watching him through the glass.

Jake nodded to the girl—a quick, silent good-bye—then turned and left.

Donatto's shoulders sagged a bit as he watched the Volkswagen back out of his driveway and tear off down the street. He walked over to the phone, where he kept a pen and a small message pad, and scribbled down the name before he forgot it. He wrote *Dylan McConnell,* and then, in larger letters which he underlined, *Red Carlyle.* He drew an equal sign between the two names and then two large question marks. He doodled aimlessly, writing over the question marks two and three times, circling the names until they looked as though they were sinking into a whirlpool. His hand ached, so he tossed down the pen.

So, Dylan McConnell and this Red Carlyle were the same man—at least, those two boys apparently thought so. Donatto tore the sheet from the pad and slipped it into his pocket next to the business card the kid had given to him. As he did, he stole another look at the card.

Misfits, Inc. Investigations.

Behind him the front door clicked shut, and Donatto smiled in spite of the circumstances. Angie had stayed outside until the boys had driven off. She liked the taller boy, the one with the blond hair. Donatto could tell. He glanced over his shoulder and watched her walk back to the sofa. She sat and began brushing the wig as she always did, only now she smoothed the brush through, and every so often she patted at the curls with the palm of her hand to make them bend the way she wanted.

"Did he ask you for your number?" he asked.

She rolled her eyes at the question and tossed the brush aside so that it clattered against the tabletop. Reaching again for the guitar, she twirled a knob on the front. Then she plugged a cable into it, and when she hit the strings a loud, jangly chord sounded through the amplifier.

"Angie," he said, "would you do that in your room, please? I—I need to make a phone call."

She placed the guitar on its stand and walked over to him. "S'okay," she said. "My stomach's a little upset from my medicine, anyway. If I lie down for a while, maybe I won't throw up."

He nodded.

When she turned toward the hallway, he saw something in the motion—maybe it was the way she tossed her head and looked at him over her shoulder, or the little skip her feet made when she turned. He couldn't put his finger on it, but for a moment she reminded him of her mother. Carole—who had left him because he never made enough money, and because he was always so tired after working construction all day.

And because she couldn't stand the guns.

Carole had died two years ago of breast cancer. First his wife's cancer; now his daughter's leukemia—leaving Donatto to wonder just what sort of world he'd been born into. One family gets the winning Lotto tickets, and another gets *this?*…

He watched Angela as she moved down the hallway. His wife was gone, he knew, but he would not lose his daughter. The doctors said it was not as bad as it seemed. They had a good record curing childhood leukemia now. When the right match came, when they found the person whose bone marrow was similar enough to Angie's, she would recover. They promised.

"Angela?" he called.

From within the shadows down the hallway, she turned and looked at him.

"He liked you too. I could tell."

She didn't say anything, just opened the door to her bedroom and stepped through. He heard it click shut behind her.

But maybe, just maybe, a smile had flickered across her face.

Donatto went back to the phone, reaching for his address book and flipping through its pages. He hadn't used it in so long—whom did he have to call except doctors?—but the number should still be here.

Thirty years since that day—and the horror that came after. It seemed impossible now that it even happened. Donatto would never forget, of course, but he had long ago come to believe that this moment, a moment when someone would once again ask questions, would never happen. He had kept a passing acquaintance with the others just in case. They never really spoke as friends, just met every few years to share drinks and tell stories. They never spoke about April 11, 1970, or mentioned the name Dylan McConnell. That was the rule. They would just drink to the time that had passed, bringing them further and further away from that day, and then they would slip each other pieces of paper bearing updated phone numbers and addresses.

Just in case.

He found it right where it belonged. Randy Harvill owned a cabin outside Missoula, Montana, and was now living the life of a hunter and fisherman. Since retiring, Randy had picked up extra money by skinning, cleaning, and butchering the deer other hunters killed, so they could stick the meat in the freezer at home like steaks they had picked up at the supermarket.

He punched in the number, and the phone began to ring. A gruff voice answered. "Yeah?"

"Randy," said Donatto. "It's me, Angelo."

A long silence followed. Donatto sensed what Randy was thinking: *He wouldn't call me. Not unless…*

"I gotta talk to you," Donatto went on. "Two guys— two high school kids—showed up at my door just now. They were asking about—you know…"

"Kids? Not law enforcement?"

"Definitely not law enforcement," Donatto replied. "They said they were working on a project, but.…" Even as he said it, he began to feel a little silly about placing the call. But then he remembered the word on the business card—*Investigations.*

"So they're writing a paper for school or something. Relax. How'd they find you?"

The question chilled Donatto. How *had* they found him? "I—I don't know," he said. "I was thinking about other things. I didn't ask. But Randy, they didn't just mention McConnell. They also asked about another guy." He reached into his pocket and fumbled for the slip of paper on which he had written the names. "Someone named Red Carlyle." His hand felt jittery; it was hard for him to hold the phone. "I think," he said, "I think—well, these kids sounded pretty sure that McConnell and this Red Carlyle are the same guy."

Another long silence. Donatto heard a faint scratching sound, and he realized Randy was scraping his fingernails across his beard. "Okay," said Randy finally, "I'm coming out there. We'll figure this out together."

Donatto nodded. "Yeah—yeah, okay. That's good."

"And there's someone else you have to call—if you can reach him. He'll be able to help even more than I can."

"Yeah, I'll do that." Donatto felt a tingle of calm try to force its way through the tension in his muscles. Randy was right. If anyone could handle this, find out what's going on—

"And *relax,*" said Randy. "There's no problem. And if there is a problem, we'll fix it." His voice dropped in volume and became more like a growl. "We'll take care of McConnell. We'll take care of these kids, if necessary. But Angelo, we need to know who they are, where they live."

Donatto slipped the business card from his pocket. Four names. And a phone number. He set the card on the countertop and tapped it with his forefinger.

"I don't think that's going to be a problem," he said.

mattie stood at Red Carlyle's door and clutched his guitar case to his chest.

Red Carlyle lived in a small frame house just outside the downtown area of Bugle Point. It was cabinlike, its siding composed of thick, overlapping planks of red cedar. A hand-painted wooden sign in the shape of a guitar hung above the doorframe; it said simply Red's Place.

The danger, Mattie knew, would be in the first second or two after he and the musician met face to face. Would Red remember him from the restaurant? Mattie would watch for a clue—a strange pause when their eyes locked, a slight drawing back of the singer's head, a narrowing of the eyes. Mattie had styled his hair differently, parting it in the middle, and he had borrowed an old pair of Byte's glasses, which he let ride at the tip of his nose so he could see over the tiny lenses. He had wanted to dye his hair platinum blond and spike it with gel, but his grandfather had told him he was going to his first guitar lesson, not a photo shoot for *Rolling Stone*.

Mattie raised his fist, drew in a breath for courage, and knocked. Red himself answered. The musician wore a T-shirt and jeans with a pair of snakeskin cowboy boots, and he held a bottle of gourmet root beer in his hand.

"Yeah, yeah, hi," Red said. "Ramiro, right? Come on in."

He has no clue, Mattie thought. If the man had recognized Mattie, he hadn't revealed it with so much as a blink.

He led Mattie through a living room filled with simple pine furniture and an ancient television set in a wood cabinet. Mattie caught a glimpse of dishes in the kitchen sink and several more root beer empties sitting on the counter.

They ended up in a room that had been converted into a full studio. Acoustic tile lined the walls and ceiling. Mattie saw a range of electronic equipment that almost made him drool—a keyboard synthesizer, a digital mixer for recording, a drum machine. A beat-up spinet piano sat against one wall, and guitars—well, guitars were everywhere. A few hung from hooks on the wall; several more rested on stands on the floor. One, its neck cracked, sat on a padded workbench. Most were acoustic steel-string guitars, the kind Mattie's grandpa called "flat-tops." A few were electric. All looked old.

In the center of the room were two chairs and a music stand.

"Let's take a look at your axe," Red offered.

Axe? Mattie wondered. *Oh, he means my guitar.*

The two sat, and Red grunted as he forced open the latches on Mattie's guitar case. When it popped open, revealing the instrument inside, Mattie felt his face heat up with embarrassment.

"*Oooooooohhh,*" Red lifted the guitar from the case the way a young father might lift his sleeping baby from its cradle. "Where did you get this?" he asked slowly, in that whisper he had, and Mattie had the sense he was talking more to himself than to anyone else. "Do you know what this is?"

Other than a guitar, no. Mattie shook his head.

"This," Red went on, "is an old Gibson el-double-ought." He held the guitar up so that Mattie could see into the sound hole. Sure enough, a faded label on the inside bore the model designation L-00, followed by a serial number. "Son, you got yourself one of the best blues guitars ever made."

"I thought it was a cheap one," Mattie admitted, tempted to believe that Red was poking fun at him.

"You kidding? Robert Johnson played a guitar like this."

Mattie shrugged. The only Robert Johnson he knew was a kindergarten classmate who used to throw sand in Mattie's face at recess. Red handed the guitar back to Mattie and moved to a small shelf of books. He grabbed one called *A History of the Blues* and flipped through its pages until he came to a photo of a smiling black man. The man wore a tight-fitting suit, a tie, and a fedora stuck at a jaunty angle on his head.

In his lap was a guitar that looked exactly like Mattie's.

"Robert Johnson," said Red. "The first, and maybe greatest, blues guitarist there ever was." He leaned over so that his nose almost touched Mattie's. "They say," he began in a hushed voice, "he played so well because he went to the crossroads at midnight and sold his soul to the devil."

Mattie felt as though his heart was shrinking to nothing inside his chest. He had sensed the word "devil" coming just before he heard it, but not soon enough to prepare for the chill it gave him.

Red slapped Mattie's shoulder. "Just an old story," he said, laughing.

"The finish is all cracked," said Mattie, turning back to his guitar. "Is it ruined?"

"It's just some 'checking.' Won't hurt the sound any," said Red. "And besides," he added, "it kinda gives the axe character, don't you think?" He smiled. Red, Mattie thought, was acting like a kid who had found a Nolan Ryan rookie card just sitting on the sidewalk outside his home. He seemed almost giddy at the sight of this old wooden…*box* Mattie was holding.

Red reached for the guitar again and struck a chord. The muffled twanging sound he had noticed at first, Mattie decided, was a little more melodic, but it still sounded like a trash can lid.

"Son," said Red, "these strings died before my granddaddy did." He reached over to the workbench and grabbed a flat, vinyl package and a piece of plastic in the shape of a small crank, which turned out to be a string-winder. Red cranked off the strings one at a time and replaced them with a new set the color of bronze. Re-stringing the instrument, clipping off the excess wire, and bringing the strings to pitch took less than ten minutes. When Red played again, the guitar sounded warm and clean. "Hear that?" said Red. "You can buy good, you can buy expensive, but you can't walk into a store and buy *old*."

Mattie understood. Red was talking about the way the aged mahogany in the guitar mellowed its tone. It sounded…*woody,* as though the strings were not steel at all, but something softer. Mattie—in spite of the fact he was nervous, in spite of what he had really come to do today—could not hold back a smile.

Red showed Mattie three chords—D, G, and A7—and started him off on some basic music theory. Mattie, in turn, found that his hand didn't want to stretch in the directions it needed to, and that the strings pressed deep, painful ruts into the tips of his fingers.

Moments before the lesson was to end, the phone rang in the other room. "Excuse me," said Red. "I better take this. Sorry."

He got up to answer it.

Mattie swallowed nervously and set the guitar down, listening to Red's footsteps disappearing down the hall. When he heard Red answer the phone, he slipped a disposable camera from his jacket pocket. He stepped back and snapped a few photos of the studio itself—he couldn't see any reason to, but who could guess what Peter might find when *he* looked at them? He moved around the room, his heart beating madly, and his ears still listened for the murmured sounds of conversation down the hall. *Nothing here,* he told himself. Tools next to the workbench. Loose guitar strings. A broken mandolin. The drawers in the small desk contained pencils, some bent paper clips, and a broken stapler that Mattie was momentarily tempted to fix. A closet revealed a vacuum cleaner, another pair of boots, a few shirts, and a shoebox tucked away on an upper shelf.

Mattie stared at it. *So why aren't the shoes on the floor with the boots?* he wondered.

He shook the box, and it rustled with papers. Mattie held his breath, his hands gripping the box, and stuck his head out the door. The muffled conversation continued in the other room: Red was scheduling a recording session, reducing his hourly price as a favor.

Mattie lifted the lid from the box. Inside were dozens of envelopes, many of them pink or other pastel colors, or decked out in stripes or prints. They looked old and faded, and the handwriting on the front was distinctly feminine. Mattie gently tugged a letter from its envelope, spread it open, and snapped a picture. He did four more the same way, not stopping to look at what the letters said, just taking photos of them and stuffing them back into the envelopes. After he photographed the fifth, he heard Red's phone conversation winding down. Seconds later, the music teacher's footsteps padded back toward the studio. Mattie scrambled. He placed the lid back on the box, but it teetered off and landed on the floor. Hissing between his teeth, he scooped the lid up, placed it on the box, and shoved the box back onto its shelf. When Red walked in, Mattie was standing next to his chair, his chest heaving and the camera hidden behind his back.

Red shrugged. "Sorry about the wait."

"Not a problem," said Mattie. He forced a smile. "So, lesson over for today?"

Red nodded. His expression didn't change. He glanced around the room, but nothing must have seemed amiss, for his body showed no visible tension.

Without Red noticing, Mattie was able to slip the camera into his guitar case as he was putting the guitar away. At least, he didn't *think* Red had seen it. The guitar teacher just stood there, swaying back and forth on his boot heels as Mattie packed up.

"Same time next week?" Mattie asked.

"Sure," said Red, eyeing him. "Sure. Next week."

Mattie fumbled in his pocket for his grandfather's check, payment for the first month of lessons. He handed it to Red, who, for a moment, looked deeply grateful to receive it before slipping it into his wallet.

"Bye," said Mattie. His grandmother would be outside, waiting in the car after doing her weekly grocery shopping. Mattie concentrated on that safe image. And as he passed Red on his way through the studio door, he clamped his eyes shut for an instant as a reminder: *Don't run. It'll look bad if you run.*

Byte printed the last of the six photos, her hand shaking as she laid it on her bed alongside the others.

"This is the worst of them," she told the other Misfits.

The photo showed a young man lying face down on the pavement, a tiny pool of blood gathering alongside his matted hair. A woman knelt above him, head turned upward, arms spread, mouth open in some terrible silent cry.

Uncle Josh was right, she thought. *They don't teach us about* this *in school.*

Peter, Jake, and Mattie were silent, their eyes scanning the photos. Peter looked at each one, then shook his head slightly before staring at the next. More than any of the others, he saw the world as a place that should *make sense.* These pictures showed him a world that didn't.

"On April 11, students held a demonstration, and the National Guard broke it up. That was the day Uncle Josh lost his leg. But Saturday was nothing compared to what happened later."

"Three exploding jeeps were *nothing?*" Mattie asked.

Byte narrowed her eyes at him. "*Shush.* Later that evening," she went on, "three hundred protesters met again on the university commons. This time they marched toward the dormitories—so they could get more people to join them—and by the time they got back to the commons there were two *thousand.*"

She pointed to a picture of a wooden building engulfed in flames. "They broke the windows of the ROTC building, and then someone set fire to it. It was old, and the university was going to demolish it anyway, okay? So the fire department showed up, but the protesters wouldn't let them work. They got in the way. They slashed the fire hoses. They threw rocks. The firemen were finally able to put the flames out, but later someone started the fire *again*. The fire department responded a second time, but that time they came with police protection. The police tear-gassed the students to drive them away from the commons. When the students retreated, the National Guard followed them. The Guardsmen placed bayonets on their rifles and charged into the crowd—driving away students, protesters, even bystanders. One Guardsman actually stabbed someone.

"The massacre…" Byte went on, speaking slowly, "happened two days later. On April 13." She'd had two days to think about all this, but her friends were hearing it for the first time. She pointed to a photo of some National Guardsmen who stood with their M-1 assault rifles raised. They were aiming to the left, but one, crouching in the center, aimed his instead at the camera. Byte looked at him, and he seemed to be looking back at her, through his sights, his finger tightening against the trigger.

"About fifteen hundred students met on the commons that Monday morning. By then everyone was ticked off. A National Guard general ordered the protesters to leave. When they refused, the Guardsmen, about 116 of them, formed what they call a 'skirmish line.'"

"Skirmish line?" asked Peter.

Byte nodded. "That's when they march in a straight line with their bayonets extended. They also fired tear gas. The protesters began to run off."

She pointed to a map of the Trenton State University campus she had printed out. "Many of them ran up this hill, called Knowledge Hill, to get away. They threw rocks at the Guardsmen; some Guardsmen threw rocks back. But basically the demonstration was over. Students wandered off to their dorms or to class; the general ordered the Guardsmen to return to the Commons."

Byte swallowed thickly and indicated the photo of the woman kneeling over the dead body. "That's when the massacre happened. Some members of the Guard, 'Troop K,' huddled together for a few moments. When they got here…" She pointed again at the map, near a building labeled Ryan Hall. "…someone ordered them to fire."

She looked at her friends, wanting to make certain they understood exactly what she was telling them. Jake leaned against the door frame, his shoulders hunched, his eyes staring into space. Mattie huddled on the corner of Byte's bed, his legs drawn up and his chin resting on his knees. He was studying the photo of the woman and the dead body. Peter stood silent, his arms folded. Two tiny creases cut into his forehead right between his eyebrows.

"About a dozen Guardsmen," Byte went on, "spun around and began firing at the students. They fired sixty-seven shots in thirteen seconds, wounding nine students…and killing four."

Her friends stared, silent.

Not knowing what else to do or say, and not caring to look at them any longer, Byte gathered the pages together and tried to slip them into one of her school folders. Her shaking hands couldn't seem to make them fit. She finally crammed them together, the corners not matching up, some of them wrinkling, and finally just tossed the folder onto her bed. She then reached for her crutches and *tack-tack-tack*ed her way over to the desk where her computer sat. Grimacing, she signed off, shut the computer down, and tossed the crutches back onto her bed. "They hurt my armpits," she said quietly and leaned her weight against the desk.

Peter looked at Jake before speaking and cleared his throat. Byte sensed that he was clearing his mind as well—of thoughts of the crying woman and the National Guardsmen with his assault rifle. "Well, Jake and I didn't learn much," he said. "We found Mr. Donatto, but he didn't know anything about Dylan McConnell—or at least that's what he said. It seemed pretty obvious that he knew more than he was telling." He looked to Jake for agreement on that last point, and Jake nodded.

"The truth was," Jake admitted, "the guy kinda scared us. We're talking *lots* of guns."

Byte looked to Mattie now. He remained huddled on her bed, but when Jake and Peter began staring at him as well, he sighed and reached for his jacket. From its pocket he removed a thick envelope from a one-hour photo lab. "I had my first lesson with Mr. Carlyle today," he mumbled. His chin was once again pressed against his knees. He tossed the envelope to Peter without another word.

Peter opened it and spread the pictures out on Byte's desktop. Jake moved to join him, and Byte, drawing a deep breath, decided it was easier to hop over rather than reach for the crutches again. Mattie remained on the bed.

"You found *letters?*" Peter nearly gasped, running his hands through the photos like they were gold pieces he'd found in his backyard.

Byte picked one up, frowning as she studied it. In one or two places, the light from the camera's flash had caught the paper at a bad angle, creating a glare that washed out the text. But Byte found that if she squinted she could read almost the entire letter.

> Dear "Red,"
>
> I miss you already. I understand why you had to go, and I understand that it hurt you as much as it hurts me, but I still ache that I didn't go with you. I know you would have tried to talk me out of it, but you wouldn't have succeeded!
>
> The world is just so crazy right now—especially in your neck of the woods—so I won't complain too much. I'll try to be understanding. When do you think you'll be coming back this way? Soon, I hope! The last…

The glare blurred the last few words. Something about a train—or maybe the word was *explain*. The signature, however, was clear enough. It said "Love, Melanie." Lingering a moment over the name, Byte set the photo down and looked again at Mattie. Her stomach twisted inside her. She felt a little as though someone had just caught her peeking into a neighbor's window. Mattie returned her gaze, and Byte understood that he felt the same way.

"They're *all* from Melanie," Mattie said. "I found two or three dozen stashed in the guy's closet."

"Hey," said Jake, "did you notice how she puts Red's name in quotation marks? Does that mean it's a nickname, or is she being clever because it's not his name at all? And what's this 'your neck of the woods' part? Why didn't she just come out and say where he's from?"

"The return address on the envelopes," said Mattie, "was in Toronto."

Peter held one of the photos, tapping it against his palm. "Hmmm, then it seems unlikely we'd be able to track this woman down after almost thirty years. But I suppose we could try calling directory assistance in Canada."

Mattie said nothing more. If anything, Byte thought, he seemed to shrink a bit at the idea of calling the woman. Peter, too, picked up on the body language. "What's the problem?" he asked.

Mattie shifted uncomfortably. "I liked the guy, Peter. He was…all right, you know? I don't know if he's this McConnell guy, but even if he is, I don't believe he tried

108 to hurt us." Mattie looked down, finding something terribly interesting on the bottom of his sneaker. He tugged absently at a loose bit of rubber. "I read those letters before I came here, and I felt like I was spying on the guy."

Peter frowned. "You *were*."

"Yeah, but it never felt this slimy before!" Mattie snapped.

Peter set the photo down. He took off his glasses and rubbed his eyes, then his swollen cheek. After thinking a minute, he put his glasses back on, pressing them into place with his forefinger. "Maybe," he said, turning to Byte, "your uncle should see those pictures you found of Trenton State."

It was a good idea. Josh had taken a few days off work and had been staying with Byte and her mom since the accident. Byte found that she liked having him in the house. It was almost like having a dad around again.

When Josh entered the room a few moments later, his eyes fell on the photos Byte had once again spread across her bed. At first he didn't recognize them, but when he saw the one of the woman kneeling over the dead body, Byte could almost feel his skin prickling. Peter picked up one of the photos and handed it to him. It was a wide-angle shot of the commons on April 11, taken by a student who had been watching the events from the roof of a nearby building. It showed some of the crowd, a handful of National Guardsmen with their rifles, and a blurred figure standing on a stage with a guitar. Dylan McConnell.

"Josh, this is the only one we have of May second," Peter said. "Where were you in relation to these people?" The other Misfits gathered around them. Byte hopped into place and leaned against Jake. She rested there, catching a whiff of his shampoo and the scent of laundry soap from his T-shirt.

"I was about here," Josh answered. "I hadn't met up with my girlfriend yet." He indicated a spot several inches off the right-hand edge of the photo.

"Okay," said Peter, pointing, "the Guardsmen are here. McConnell's here. I can see one of the jeeps over there, and—wait a minute." He jabbed his finger somewhere down on the photo, right in the middle of the crowd. "What's this? Is this woman taking *pictures?*"

Mattie shook his head. "The contraption she's holding is too big—and it's the wrong shape. Looks more like a home movie camera, Peter."

"There's *film* of this somewhere?" Peter exulted.

Josh tore the photo from Peter's hand and held it up for a closer look. He stared at it for a very long time before he whispered a single word.

It sounded like "Luuuna."

chapter seven

Monday, 8:00 A.M.
Federal Bureau of Investigation:
Bugle Point Office

With his close-shaven head, football player's build, flat voice, and masklike expression, Special Agent Robert Polaski projected the image of a man with no sense of humor at all. And in truth, he had none.

So when Nick Braddock pushed through the door of his office, he raised an eyebrow at the sight of Polaski grinning at him. Nick's fellow agent—and sometime partner—leaned back in his chair, smiling, with his hands folded across his abdomen. He twiddled his fingers up and down.

"What's with you?" Nick asked.

Polaski jerked his head in the direction of the bureau chief's office. "Washington sent you a baby-sitter."

Nick moved to his cubicle and set down his briefcase, all the while focusing on the frosted glass walls that set off the office of Curtis Whitecloud. The agents called Whitecloud "the Chief," a play on his Bureau title as well as his Native American heritage. Through the dull glass,

Nick could see Whitecloud talking to another man, who appeared to be standing at attention. The Chief gestured to a chair, Nick saw, but the other man did not move.

A moment later the office door opened. Whitecloud stuck his head out and looked in Nick's direction. "Agent Braddock," he said, "I need to see you a moment, please."

"Ooooohhh," muttered Polaski under his breath, "Agent *Braddock.*"

Nick frowned at Polaski as he passed him.

Whitecloud's office was spartan, the desktop clean except for a blotter and a stapler. On a side table, next to Whitecloud's printer, was a brass paperweight. The agents in the office had given it to the Chief after Whitecloud had been shot during a major kidnapping case. It was shaped like a heart, with a lightning-bolt break cutting through the center. Glued into the break was a .45 caliber bullet. Below the heart, engraved at its base, were the words "Too big a target to miss."

Nick noticed that the newcomer in the office kept glancing at the paperweight. The man's face betrayed little, but Nick thought he picked up a hint of disapproval. He was surprised at the intense dislike he suddenly felt for the man.

"Special Agent Braddock," said Whitecloud, "this is Special Agent Paul Bonhoffer from headquarters. He has the information you requested."

He's delivering it personally? Nick thought. That might explain all the hoops Nick had to jump through to get the material. Bonhoffer stuck out his hand, his face expressionless, and gripped Nick's in a tight, formal handshake.

"Pleasure to work with you," he said. His words were precise, clipped like a well-trimmed lawn.

Nick stiffened. *Work with me?*

Bonhoffer looked to be in his early fifties. Like Polaski's, his hair was shaved to the length of a tooth-brush bristle, but the front was spiked up with some kind of 1950s-style hair cream.

"I just requested a file," said Nick flatly.

The agent from Washington stared at him. The corners of his mouth ticked upward for an instant, then settled back down. Nick wondered if the man had smiled.

"I've been gathering information about Dylan McConnell for well over twenty years," Bonhoffer said, "while *you* were still struggling through pre-law, I believe." His eyes narrowed, the gesture measurable, per-haps, only with a microscope. "Like it or not, Special Agent Braddock…" The title dripped off his tongue. "…you caught my attention. Whatever you learn about McConnell, I intend to learn as well."

The Chief had taken his place behind his desk. His eyes flickered back and forth between the two men. For sev-eral seconds, a pencil twirled in his fingers. "Well," he said finally, "since you two have hit it off so famously, I'm sure you're quite capable of continuing your work somewhere other than my office." He motioned with his head to the door, and Bonhoffer exited.

Nick paused before leaving. Whitecloud looked at him and shrugged. "Next time you need something from

Washington," he suggested, "just ask 'em to stick it in the mail."

Nick nodded, closing the door behind him.

Bonhoffer walked as a soldier marches—shoulders straight, left arm swinging rhythmically. From his right arm dangled a designer Italian briefcase, which he set on top of Nick's desk. The heavy latches clicked solidly as he opened it. "Shall we begin?" he said. It didn't sound like a question.

Nick pulled up an extra chair. An image of Peter flashed in his mind. *I love you, son,* he thought, *but what in heaven's name have you gotten me into now?*

Byte jumped when the phone rang. She stared down at it, hesitating. The conversation would be difficult.

Uncle Josh had refused to place the call himself. He explained that Luna had disappeared the day he lost his leg. She had gone straight home and transferred to another university. She had never written or called to apologize. Josh learned later that she had phoned the hospital to make sure he was all right, but she had not asked to be put through to his room. Now, thirty years later, Josh could only tell Byte that Kathleen Keillor— Luna—had arrived at Trenton State from some small town in Nebraska, and that he thought her father's name was Edgar. Nebraska had only three area codes, so Byte checked Internet phone listings for each one. She found no listing for a *Keillor, Edgar* in any of them. She tried again, this time searching for *any* listings under the name Keillor. She found three. After trying each several times, Byte found that two of them were dead ends.

The third turned out to belong to Lawrence Keillor, Edgar's older brother. Luna's uncle.

Lawrence wasn't quite sure where Kathleen—he called her Katie—was living now, but Edgar and Mary had moved to Florida for the weather. Byte told him her uncle was an old college friend of their daughter, and he gave Byte their number. When Byte reached Edgar, he hemmed and hawed, refusing to pass along his daughter's number. Byte finally got him to agree to pass along a message. She gave her number and said, "Tell her I'm calling for Joshua Quinn."

That was ten minutes ago. Now the Caller ID indicated that someone in Florida was calling her back.

Byte snatched up the handset. "Hello?"

"I—I'm returning a call from a Eugenia Salzmann." The woman sounded weary, doubtful. Byte heard a baby crying in the background. "I'm sorry," she said, "I'm baby-sitting my granddaughter."

"Kathleen Keillor?" asked Byte.

"Yes." More hesitation. "That was my maiden name."

Byte explained that she was Joshua Quinn's niece and that she was doing "research"—that was the way she put it—on the events at Trenton State. She didn't exactly say she was working on a project for school, but she figured it wouldn't hurt if the woman chose to make that assumption. She then told the woman about the photograph and how her uncle had recognized his old friend, Luna.

The woman laughed at her old name. "Oh, for heaven's *sake*." She sounded almost flattered to be remembered after so long.

Byte closed her eyes and drew in a deep breath, her free hand closed into a fist. "So," she went on cheerily, "I was wondering if you still had the film you were shooting that day and if I could borrow it."

"Why, yes, I suppose I do somewhere," said the woman. "I never throw anything away. It may take a little time to find it. You know, to go through boxes." She paused. Then, as if it were an afterthought, she added quietly, "How *is* Joshua, by the way?"

"He's fine," said Byte.

"Tell him," said the woman, "well—tell him Katie says she's sorry."

"I will," said Byte.

The woman brightened then. "So," she said more quickly, "are you in a hurry for the film? If I can find it, would you like me to send it overnight?"

Byte smiled.

Tuesday evening
Maggio's Italian Restaurant

It was almost terrifying, Donatto thought, how easy it had been to find Red Carlyle.

Randy Harvill stared over his plate of food at Angelo. After a moment he stopped eating, his fork clattering to the tabletop. "There's no point sweating this," he said. "Either this guy is McConnell, or he's not." He leaned forward in his chair, his elbows resting on the table. Grimacing, he squeezed his hands into fists so that all the knuckles crackled at once.

Randy hadn't aged well since Angelo last saw him. He still had the same long, sticklike legs—and the potbelly that drooped over the silver belt buckle he'd won in a rodeo in 1974. Only now Randy's narrow chest seemed to have caved in a little, and every so often he bent forward and coughed fiercely. His face had aged from wrinkled to craggy, browned by sunlight in the high elevations of Montana. Angelo had hardly recognized him when he stepped off the plane.

"Y'ask me," he went on, "McConnell's dead. Live a life on the run like that, you don't live very long."

Angelo ignored the comment. *Yes,* he thought, *it had been frighteningly easy.* He had found Red Carlyle listed in the phone directory. When he called the number—to hear the voice, he had to hear the voice—he got an answering machine telling him Red was not home. He could not tell if the voice belonged to McConnell, but the recorded message referred interested guitar students to another number and an ad in the Yellow Pages. Angelo called that number and got another taped message, this one informing him that Red Carlyle was performing every Tuesday through Saturday.

Here. At Maggio's.

Angelo and Randy had arrived half an hour early, taking seats in the smoking section, far away from the stage. After they ordered, Carlyle came in and started setting up his equipment. Angelo tried to watch the singer without *appearing* to watch, but he found he couldn't turn away.

Randy whispered, "It's him."

Angelo wasn't as certain. Carlyle's hair was coppery rather than the dark brown of Dylan McConnell's, but that could be a dye job. The hair was shorter, too, and the beard less scraggly. Angelo listened as Red Carlyle began to sing. He would never forget McConnell's tenor whine. This voice was close, but not a perfect match. Then again, who could tell how a voice might change after thirty years?

Most importantly, Angelo saw something in Carlyle's face—in the wrinkles around the eyes, maybe. He struggled for several moments before he recognized it. It was *pain*—the pain of loss. Angelo saw it when he looked in the mirror each morning, and he understood why a man who had spent his life in hiding might have such a look.

"It's *him*," Randy repeated.

Though no longer hungry, Angelo reached for a breadstick and broke it in half. He left the two halves sitting on his plate. "Maybe."

Randy reached across the table and grasped Angelo's wrist. As weak as he looked, his grip hurt. "It's McConnell," he hissed. "I'd recognize him anywhere."

"If it is him," Angelo said, "what do we do about it?"

Red Carlyle was singing a love song.

Randy glanced around the restaurant before speaking again. "It would be different if we had just run into the

118 guy somewhere," said Randy, "we wouldn't have to do anything. No one would know we'd found him." He was still gripping Angelo's arm. Angelo yanked it away. "But who are these kids you talked about? What do they want?"

More importantly, what do they know? Angelo wondered.

"If the police—or worse, the FBI—get in on this," Randy went on, "we could have trouble."

"McConnell's been quiet for thirty years," offered Angelo. On the stage, Red Carlyle's eyes were closed. The singer shook his head back and forth as he sang.

"If someone's investigating him, he may not have a choice," said Randy. "Speaking of the police," said Randy, "and the…well, have you called—"

"Yeah yeah yeah," said Angelo, cutting him off. He didn't want to hear the name.

"He can *help* us," Randy insisted. "He's been more on top of this than either of us. He can control this, maybe."

Angelo waved off the idea, but he knew his friend was right.

The two men sat quietly in their dark corner, their eyes locked on the stage. The singer was blowing into a harmonica—a long, drawn-out moan over his gentle fingerpicking. *It could be him*, Angelo thought. *The hair, the voice, the eyes.*

"We have to do something," Randy pleaded. "I was twenty-five years in the military, Angelo. I got a good pension. I'm not gonna lose it because some longhair radical bleeding heart peacenik took it in his head to blow up a jeep thirty years ago."

"You were there," Angelo reminded him. "You know it's not that simple."

That silenced Harvill. He grabbed a crust of garlic bread and used it to mop up the sauce on his plate. Head down, he stuffed the bread into his mouth and chewed, dusting his fingers over his empty salad bowl.

"Randy," said Angelo, softening, "we have to know for sure it's McConnell before we…before we do anything."

Randy wiped his forearm across his mouth. "We gotta shut McConnell up—"

"If he *is* McConnell," Angelo interjected.

"We gotta find out what those kids know, and we gotta deal with them before they learn anything more…anything dangerous," said Randy. "Lemme see that card."

Angelo fished into his pocket for the business card the Braddock kid had given him. He remembered the way the kid had asked his questions—flat, to the point, like the cops on TV. He seemed to know what he was doing. Angelo slid the card across the table, then reached over and tapped his finger on Peter's name. "This is the one we need to work on," he said.

His friend regarded the names on the card, then flicked it back to Angelo, shaking his head. "No," he told him. "This Eugenia Salzmann—the girl. We start with her."

chapter eight

Tuesday, fifth period
Bugle Point High School

bringgg! *Bringgg! Bringgg!* Peter rolled his eyes and reached for his backpack. On his desktop was his copy of Counter-Point, the Bugle Point High School newspaper. He picked it up and stuffed it under his arm as he rose from his desk.

His classmates laughed and chattered as they lined up at the door. Mr. Blair shook his head—a major show of irritation by the chemistry teacher's usual standards, Peter thought—and swung open the door to let the herd out.

Peter agreed with his teacher. This was getting annoying.

Four times today the fire alarm bell had rung. Four times students had sauntered from their classes in the middle of the period to meet in the center of the campus, standing in small clusters while their teachers muttered and tried to take roll. When the first alarm went off, no one had much of anything to say. One paradox of school life was that *surprise* fire drills were *expected.* But the second drill was a genuine surprise; the third was astonishing, the fourth…well, by the fourth, students had begun to laugh. A few of the bigger idiots pumped their fists at the idea of another interruption. Others—even some of the more sensible members of the student council—nodded their heads in faint agreement with the statement someone was trying to make. It had all happened so fast, like a match touched to a pile of dry leaves.

This morning's *Counter-Point* featured a front-page article about the book banning. The article listed the books Principal Steadham had removed and the reasons behind the removal, then finished with a bombshell: Ms. Langley's resignation. Page four carried a scathing editorial about the ban, accompanied by a student-drawn cartoon of Steadham in a firefighter's uniform, setting fire to a pile of books with one hand, a copy of *Fahrenheit 451* in the other. Peter had laughed aloud at the clever reference. *Fahrenheit 451* was Ray Bradbury's famous novel about a world where a handful of people had memorized entire books to preserve them, because the authorities had burned the books themselves out of existence.

Someone pushed open the glass doors leading to the quad area, and Peter, caught in the stream of students, found himself swept outside.

As early as first period he had sensed that the article had blindsided Mr. Steadham. Peter had passed by the office earlier and heard the man yelling, seen the principal's face sweaty and flushed. Surely Mrs. Forrestal, the faculty advisor for the newspaper, had told Steadham about the upcoming article and offered him a chance to comment. Peter surmised that Steadham had been too arrogant to believe that she would have the nerve to allow students to print anything so controversial. Perhaps he had even threatened her, but Mrs. Forrestal had taught at the school nearly as long as Steadham had been alive. She was also a four-time County Teacher of the Year and a one-time National Teacher of the Year. She'd have to commit a felony, Peter figured, before anyone would dare fire her.

And years ago, Ms. Langley had been her student.

Not long after the distribution of the school paper, someone had pulled the fire alarms, disrupting classes and frustrating the new principal. It was probably an anonymous act of protest against the book banning. Indeed, as the day passed, Peter sensed the passions increasing, coming nearer to a boil, every time the alarm rang. The tone around school was one of hushed whispers—which seemed far more real and intense than the general loud bellyaching that followed most school policy decisions.

A shadow loomed from behind Peter. A familiar voice said, "Read any good books lately?"

It was Jake.

Peter snorted. Then came a fleeting thought: *I am enjoying* Stranger in a Strange Land. *If I had waited a day longer to check it out,* he wondered, *would I have found it on the shelf?*

Byte and Mattie huddled together a few yards away, so Peter and Jake strode over to join them. Mattie tossed M&Ms high into the air, trying to catch them in his mouth. One bounced off his front teeth and landed in the dirt. Byte surveyed the crowd, a hint of a frown on her face.

"What are you thinking?" Peter asked.

Byte didn't answer. She didn't seem entirely sure *how* to answer. She appeared to be mulling over her own ideas about the false fire alarms.

Just then a very long bell sounded—*brrrrriiiiii-innnnnggg*—an "all-clear" signal ordering students back to class. Most of them, Peter and his friends included, moved in that direction, but many held back. Mr. Steadham stood at the edge of the quad, glaring at the crowd. He held a bullhorn in one hand and waved toward the building with the other, hurrying the students along. Some people, however, were not moving. A few—a handful—sat down silently on the grass. A few more saw them, paused, looked at one another as though measuring their resolve, then sat down with them. Soon more and more sat. Those who had started toward the building realized what was happening and moved back to the quad, joining them.

Peter saw a flicker of doubt cross his friends' faces. What would be the consequence of joining this silent demonstration? Byte was the first to decide that she didn't care. She sat, staring at Peter, and he knew that if he sat down with her, Jake and Mattie would sit as well.

Peter scooted to the ground.

Mr. Steadham raised the bullhorn. "Return to your classes," he called out. "There will be severe penalties for any student who does not return to class."

No one moved. Almost the entire student body, nearly two thousand people, had migrated to the quad. Peter heard little conversation—and no laughter at all. Teachers stood by, some ordering their students back to the building. Most remained silent. A few looked to Mr. Steadham to take control, barely able to conceal the smiles that seemed to tickle at the corners of their mouths.

Mr. Steadham fumed, his face flushing. He raised the bullhorn again. "Return to your classes immediately!" His shouting into the bullhorn made the resulting sound dull and staticky. From somewhere in the throng of students, a can of 7-Up flew in a high arc toward the principal, spraying liquid as it tumbled in the air. For a few brief seconds, the sunlight caught the spray and made a rainbow.

"This is getting interesting," said Jake.

"Wanna watch me make a principal disappear?" Mattie offered.

Byte's smile was wide and brimming with satisfaction. "Guys," she said quietly, "looks like we have ourselves a protest."

The Bugle Point High School Student Handbook stated the rule in boldfaced letters: **Pagers and cellular**

phones are not permitted on campus and will be con-fiscated. Every student knew the rule, and on any given day about 5 percent of the student body routinely ignored it.

So it was no surprise to Peter when a news van from the local NBC affiliate pulled into the parking lot, a Channel 5 truck following right behind it. Peter nudged Byte and gestured toward the trucks. She nodded her approval.

A few print reporters had arrived as well. Peter spotted one man walking briskly toward the main office. He held a notepad in one hand and a tiny cassette recorder in the other. He also saw Rebecca Kaidanov, a reporter for the *Bugle Point Courier.* Not long ago she had helped the Misfits in their efforts to prevent the slaughter of an endangered species of kingfisher. On her way into the office, Rebecca waved at the Misfits, then swept her hand broadly across the sea of students as if to ask *is this your work?*

The crowd grew quiet. One student whispered to the next, and the word passed along. It was like the children's game, telephone—only here everyone seemed to be getting the message: *Be absolutely quiet. Say nothing.*

In a few seconds, two thousand students squared their shoulders, faced front, and closed their mouths. The whispering that had been going on since the protest began faded now to a deadly silence.

One minute.

Two minutes.

Peter thought the sheer number of people, combined with the eerie silence, felt unnatural. It was as though he had suddenly gone deaf at a pep rally. Incidental sounds seemed amplified: a plastic cup skittering across the pavement, a breeze rustling a tree branch, the explosive punch of the crash bar on the building's glass doors when Principal Steadham poked his head outside for another look. After a few minutes, police cars entered the school, their lights on but their sirens off. When the officers shut down their engines, they left the lights turning, adding to the freakish atmosphere.

The media picked up on the change. The reporter for Channel 5 tugged on her microphone wire and ran her fingers through her hair. She repeated to her crew, "Are we up? Are we up?" Rebecca and the other print reporter hurried out of the building, sensing that something was happening. Impossibly, the silence went on for twenty minutes. Mr. Steadham came out of the building and yelled at the students, demanding that they return to class. His voice sounded ridiculously loud against the background of silence, and he gazed in terror at the news cameras and pushed his way back into the building.

Another ten minutes passed.

When Steadham returned, he huddled with the police officers—no doubt trying to find out what they were going to do to get his school back under control. Peter grinned. The police were here to keep the peace, and the students were, if nothing else, peaceful. Steadham went back inside and did not come out again.

"I don't know how much longer I can keep quiet like this," Mattie muttered. Byte swatted him on the knee.

The silence continued for several more minutes, but Peter felt a change in the mood of the crowd. The silence was becoming restless. He heard braying laughter. Suddenly a chunk of rock flew across the quad and shattered a classroom window. Another followed, striking the office doors and splintering the glass. Someone in the crowd pushed someone else—perhaps the person who had thrown the rocks—and sent him sprawling. Someone else threw a fist.

In an instant two boys, then three, then four, were rolling around in the grass with arms flailing. Elsewhere in the crowd, a girl's voice shouted a nasty word—probably at the fighters. Another girl took offense and slapped her. Now the two girls were going at it, scratching each other and pulling each other's hair until they, too, lay rolling in the grass, screaming their anger even though they were nose to nose.

The police sprinted into the crowd with drawn billy clubs. Students scattered to get out of the way. Peter hauled Byte to her feet, looking for the quickest path of escape. Mattie grabbed her crutches, and Jake picked her up to carry her out of a policeman's path. The cop, assuming Jake was attacking Byte, skidded to a stop and raised his club, preparing to swing it against Jake's exposed back. Peter watched breathless as Jake turned and backpedaled a few steps with one raised, open palm. The cop saw the gesture, looked momentarily at Byte's cast, nodded, then moved on.

In moments, the silence had turned into a tidal wave of noise. Students screamed and ran, finding safety by the football field or near the gym. The afternoon school buses arrived and their drivers stared in fascination at the violence. Some students ran towards the buses, seeking shelter. A wall of bodies five or six people thick encircled the brawling students. Some people screamed, urging the fighters on. *Hit 'im! Hit 'im in the face!* The police, as well as some faculty members, pulled the students away one at a time. Several resisted and received a truncheon blow across the shoulders. One boy—one very foolish boy, Peter thought—actually pushed a cop and received a solid blow across the back of the head. He staggered off, blood trailing behind his ear and across his neck.

Throughout all this, Byte leaned against Jake, her arm circled around his back. Peter watched her study the melee. She bit her lip and crinkled her nose to set her glasses straight. A few moments ago, Peter thought, she had surveyed the demonstration as if it were a birthday present she'd been waiting for all year. Now she looked as though she had opened the present only to find that the box was empty.

"Are you all right?" Peter asked.

Byte shook her head without saying anything. The protest had started out as a harmless yet potent way for students to silently shout their support for Ms. Langley. The protest had been thrilling. But it had turned into a childish and frightening display of violence. To make a point, and to help Ms. Langley, Byte would have willingly suffered a shot from a billy club herself. Now, sadly, the clubs had come anyway, and the only point students had made was that teens were immature and irresponsible. Worse, they had made it even harder for someone to try again.

Byte sagged against Jake. He was all that was holding her up. "It's ruined," she said. "We could have done something—something really good—and now it's ruined."

Jake drove Byte home. He opened the car door for her and then walked beside her as she shuffled toward the house on her crutches.

"I'll see you later," he said.

"Bye," she said.

Just as he turned back toward his car, Byte surprised herself by throwing her arms around Jake's neck. Her crutches clattered to the ground. She could feel him hesitate, but then he circled his own strong arms around her back. They stood there, holding each other and swaying back and forth. Byte was the first to pull away. She stepped back, her face flushed, and waited while Jake picked up her crutches. She shuffled inside, closing the door gently behind her. A moment later—a long moment, it seemed, one in which it was a little hard to breathe—she heard Jake's footsteps walking away. Byte listened with her eyes closed.

Josh lounged on the living room couch, a book splayed open in his hand. He turned his head slowly in her direction, a flat and impenetrable expression on his face.

"How was your day?" he asked.

"Same old same old," said Byte.

He gestured toward the dining table, the place where the mail usually ended up. "You got a package from FedEx," he said, and turned back to his book.

Fully recovered now from her moment with Jake, Byte moved to the table as quickly as the crutches would carry her. Sitting among a pile of bills, credit card offers, and catalogs, was a padded envelope from Kathleen Keillor.

She snatched up the package and rushed to the door, her crutches jouncing painfully under her arms. When she threw the door open, she saw Jake's Escort backing out of the driveway.

"Jake!" she screamed. She waved the envelope. "Jake!"

The car stopped in the middle of the street, and the driver's side window cranked down.

"Wait a sec!" Byte shouted.

She turned back into the house, swinging on the crutches past her uncle, down the hallway, and into her mother's bedroom. Hanging from a peg in the closet was her mom's digital video camera. Byte grabbed it, slung the strap over her shoulder, and started back toward the front door of the house. Halfway there she decided it was easier and less painful to hop on her one good leg than it was to use the stupid crutches. She held them with one arm as she hobbled to the door.

Jake was still waiting. When he saw her coming, he leaped out and helped her to his car—holding the crutches in one hand and keeping her steady with the other. Grunting with the effort, Byte slipped into the back seat, the only place she could fit—considering she had one leg that wouldn't bend.

"You know that huge camera store in the mall?" she asked, breath bursting from her.

"Uh huh."

"You can take old home movies there and have them converted onto regular VHS, right?"

"Think so," said Jake.

Byte leaned forward and patted his cheek with her hand. "You're my hero."

Peter ignored the way his dad's guest glared at him. Something about Agent Paul Bonhoffer made the back of Peter's neck prickle. Even as the man "relaxed" on the sofa, he looked as though—well, as though his spine didn't bend. With his bristly hair and that weird dab of styling grease in the front, he looked like a G.I. Joe figure that had gone out of production around 1952. Peter's foot tapped angrily against the floor. *I hate the guy's attitude. It's like he thinks he outranks my dad or something.*

Peter forced back a smile when he remembered their earlier conversation. Bonhoffer had opened a hefty file on Dylan McConnell, then looked up at Peter, who was leaning in the doorway. Peter smiled and waved.

"Shouldn't your son be doing his homework instead of sticking his nose in FBI business?" Bonhoffer had asked.

Nick Braddock hadn't even looked up from the paperwork laid out before him. "Sticking his nose in FBI business *is* my son's homework," he replied.

Five minutes later the call had come from Jake and Byte. They had picked up Mattie and were on their way over.

Peter heard them now. Jake's Escort swung into the Braddock driveway, its tires squealing. When Peter turned on the porch light and opened the door, he found Byte grinning at him. Jake and Mattie stood braced on either side of her to keep her from getting wobbly.

She waved a videotape in front of Peter's nose. "Wanna see a movie?"

"We got film of Trenton State!" Jake said.

"Got any popcorn?" asked Mattie.

Hauling Byte up the stairs to Peter's room took a solid five minutes. She went up backwards, Peter and Jake on either side of her, raising her one step at a time. One…two…three…*lift!*

Once upstairs, though, Byte was a flurry of motion. She unplugged the cables from the back of the VCR and plugged them into the digital video camera. Then she connected another set of wires from the video camera to Peter's television.

"I get it," Peter said. "Now the videotape's going through the videocam before it gets to the TV. You're making a digital copy of the film as it plays."

"Thank you, Mr. Wizard," said Mattie.

Byte stabbed a button on the VCR with a finger, and a moment later images began playing across the TV screen. A man with longish hair and a bushy mustache grinned idiotically, waving a hello to the camera.

Byte burst out laughing. "Oh, my *gawd!* That's Uncle Josh! He'd die if he saw this!"

The images were jerky, bouncing around each time the camera moved, sometimes going out of focus, and sometimes showing the ground or a building.

Or a line of National Guardsmen holding assault rifles.

Peter, Jake, and Mattie scooted closer to the television.

Now the camera swung around again, a wide sweeping arc that blurred the images and colors until it came to a stop. It settled on a man holding a guitar and standing at a microphone. Clearly the man was singing, but the only sound that came through the speakers was a faint hiss. Eight-millimeter home movies from 1970 didn't come with audio.

"Dylan McConnell," Peter whispered.

Mattie moved even closer and squinted at the screen.

The camera stayed on McConnell for several long moments. The image was not very large—McConnell was several yards away and standing on a platform—but Peter compared the man on the screen with his memories of the man he'd seen in Maggio's. "The hair color's different," he said.

Jake frowned. "His height and, well, his posture seem sort of like the guy in the restaurant," he suggested.

"You can't say that for sure," said Mattie. "Film can fool

you. This guy could be six inches tall and the stage could be a shoebox."

The camera swung away again, settling once more on the line of National Guardsmen. Around them were members of the crowd, their faces twisted in anger. One guy dressed in a black T-shirt and psychedelic bell-bottoms raised his middle finger toward one of the Guardsmen, and the soldier glared back stonily.

Then all hell broke loose.

Something happened and the crowd surged forward. It seemed to Peter that the line separating the two groups disappeared. The camera jittered so much that it was hard to make out anything—blurs of color, flashes of a face, a fist, a club, someone falling to the ground. The camera swung around again, now settling on some soldiers standing in the distance, firing canisters that trailed white smoke. One Guardsman stepped toward the camera, holding his palm out to cover the lens, but he pulled away as the gas landed.

People had scattered. The image on the screen was bouncing. "Luna" must have been running, holding the camera trigger down as she did. She aimed the camera at the retreating crowd, behind which—and barely visible—were three National Guard jeeps. Peter watched, fascinated, as one by one the jeeps exploded. A huge fireball rose from the last explosion, bursting like a mini-sun and rising out of the picture.

More blurred, jittery images. More running. The ground suddenly leaped up, and a jagged line formed across the picture, a black lightning bolt from top to bottom. Luna had dropped the camera, and the lens had broken. It then swung up—she must have reached down to grab it—and the picture went black.

The Misfits stared silently at the blank screen for a very long moment. Peter was the first to speak, his voice thick. "Run it back to just before the jeeps explode," he said. "I want my dad to see this."

He ran downstairs for his father, and, of course, Agent Bonhoffer came up as well. Mr. Braddock introduced him to the Misfits. While Byte explained what the film was and how she had acquired it, Bonhoffer remained silent, but he tugged at his nose several times with thumb and forefinger, almost glaring at her. Peter felt waves of anger coming off the man like waves of heat off asphalt in summer.

Peter also noticed that, while he'd been gone, Byte had disconnected the videocam and slipped it back into its case. Now she sat on the corner of Peter's bed, the case partially hidden behind her back. Peter looked at her and she raised an eyebrow in reply.

"Mr. Braddock," said Mattie, "take a look and tell us what you think." He had rewound the video; now the images once again played across the television screen. Mr. Braddock brought his face closer to the screen as the jeeps exploded.

"Run it again," he said.

Mattie wound it back and let the tape run again.

"What do you think, Paul—er, Agent Bonhoffer?" asked Mr. Braddock.

"We have the statements from the investigators at the

time," Bonhoffer said. "This is nothing new. We know already that someone—probably McConnell—placed a pipe bomb under each jeep."

Peter saw his father frown. "Run it again."

As the film ran, Mr. Braddock pointed at the screen when the jeeps exploded. "See that?" he said. "See that? The first one to go is the one in the middle. Now why wouldn't the bombs go off at the same time? They were radio-controlled, right? One radio signal, three explosions."

Before Peter's dad could say more, Bonhoffer stepped forward. He punched the eject button on the VCR, and when it spat out the tape, he grabbed it. "Thank you," he said, his smile like a crack running through old wood. "You've done good work. The FBI lab will need to examine this, of course. I assume you have the original film as well? I'll take that, too." Then he held out his hand. The tips of his fingers twitched.

Byte cleared her throat, and slowly raised her own hand, palm out. "Ummm—s'cuse me," she said. "The film and the videotape are mine, right? I mean, don't you have to have a warrant or something if you're going to take them away from me?"

Under his breath, Mattie said, "Easy, girl. You can't walk on crutches if you're hands are cuffed."

Peter just folded his arms, waiting for Bonhoffer to answer Byte's question.

"Very true," said the FBI agent. He was smiling now at Peter's dad, as if the two shared some kind of secret. Peter's father did not smile back. "Of course, a warrant would list everything having to do with the film or film recording." He ticked items off on his fingers. "We'd confiscate the film, the videotape, your cameras, your VCR, every videotape in your house, your television, and, of course, any computer."

He stopped there. His hand hung out there again, waiting. Byte gripped the nylon bag containing her laptop.

Peter looked to his dad for help, but Mr. Braddock said nothing. Byte crinkled her nose to set her glasses straight, sighed, then reached into the outside pocket on her computer bag. She removed a cardboard box and handed it to Bonhoffer. The agent, nodding his approval, lifted the lid of the box and took out a plastic reel that was perhaps three-and-a-half inches in diameter. He rolled off a foot or two of film and held it up to the light.

"Excellent," he said. "Excellent. Thank you." His eyes narrowed as he stared down at Byte. "You didn't make a second videotape of this film, did you, hmmm?"

Byte shook her head with wide-eyed innocence. "Oh, no *sir*," she said. Bonhoffer didn't reply. He just turned and left the room. Nick Braddock followed, glancing over his shoulder and shrugging as he closed the door behind him.

A long moment of silence followed. Mattie stared at Byte, his jaw hanging open. "Byte!" he hissed. "You just lied to the FBI!"

"Did not," Byte said.

"You said you didn't make another copy of the film," Mattie insisted. "But you did! You made one on that digital videocam."

Byte reached for the bag containing the camera and clutched it to her chest. "I did not lie," she said. "I told him I didn't make a *second videotape*." The innocent look played across her face again as she stared first at Peter, then Jake, then Mattie, daring each to challenge her.

Peter leaned back in his chair. *I'm going to have to marry this girl*, he thought.

When she got home, Byte's first impulse was to throw down the video camera and flop into bed. Instead, she took it out of the bag and connected its cables to an input jack on her desktop computer. Once the computer was up and running, she saved the digitized film by burning it onto a CD-ROM disk.

On the computer screen, the film seemed even more awkward, the people jerking around like tiny puppets. But Byte could do things with the film in this digitized form that she could never do with a videotape. When Dylan McConnell appeared, she keyed in a command and a bright red square appeared around McConnell's head. She used the mouse to grab the corners of the square, adjusting its size so that McConnell's face was perfectly centered. When she clicked inside the square, the face leaped out and filled the entire screen, its details blurred and indistinct.

Byte keyed in another command. *Enhance.*

The image on the screen broke into hundreds of colored pixels that flitted around like tiny insects. When they stopped, Byte could make out the line of Dylan McConnell's nose, the wrinkling at the corner of his mouth, the color of his eyes. *Hello,* she thought, and then she hit *Print.*

Now she studied the rest of the film—the beatings, the clouds of gas, the explosions—and watched for anything else that looked interesting.

Something did.

Just before the whole troop stormed into the crowd, one of the National Guardsmen made a gesture with his hand. He raised it and flicked his index finger in the direction of the protesters. That gesture, Byte figured, had been the order to move in.

So, you're the guy in charge, huh?

She worked her magic with the computer again, selecting the area around the man's head, adjusting the square around it. Click and enhance. The colored pixels flickered, and when they settled Byte saw a clear image of the man's face.

She drew closer to the screen, her heart pounding.

At first she couldn't make sense of what she was seeing. The image was too far from anything she'd expected. She looked again. The face. The nose. Those eyes. The hair. She couldn't be mistaken.

Without taking her eyes off the screen she reached for the phone to call Peter. Her finger bounced off the buttons clumsily, and she had to try a second and third time before the number actually began to ring.

"Hullo?"

It was Peter, his voice dull with sleep.

"Peter," said Byte, "I can't believe this. I don't know what it means." She was talking too fast. She could sense that much. She'd have to slow down if she was going to make him understand. Catching her breath, she told him how she had isolated and enhanced the faces of the two men.

"And then I saw him, Peter. The Guardsman. I *saw* him."

"Saw *who?*" Peter asked.

Byte had to again force herself to stop, to breathe. "It was *him*," she said. "It was the guy at your house tonight. The FBI agent. Paul Bonhoffer."

Thursday

today they would practice shooting. Donatto flipped
through his keys until he found the tiny brass one
that opened the rifle cabinet. He reached for the
Remington, the one with the filigree carved on the barrel
and the image of a deer formed in gold on the stock. The
gun felt heavy but well balanced in his hand. He held it
a moment—resisting the urge to stare down its sight at
the couch or the kitchen sink or the mailbox outside,
just for the way it would feel—before passing it to
Randy.

"Beautiful," said Harvill. Donatto watched as his
friend held the gun up and stared through its scope at
Angie's cat. The cat eyed him warily, drawing itself up
from the carpet and leaping into a chair.

Angelo took a box of shells from a locked desk drawer,
the cardboard sides of the box caving in slightly from the
pressure of his fingers. Had he and Randy been planning
a hunting trip—up to the mountains for deer, or to the

lake for duck—Donatto would have picked up the shells without a thought, but this time he held on to them for a moment. Randy reached for them, and Angelo gave the box to him without saying a word.

Randy sat on the couch and set the box on the coffee table in front of him. He took out three or four shells and loaded them into the rifle, nodding at the clean, mechanical *snick* when they entered.

"How long since you've been to a rifle range?" asked Harvill.

"Couple years," said Angelo. "Went hunting last spring, though."

Randy ran an oilcloth along the rifle's wooden stock and grip. "Went by his house last night."

Donatto felt his skin tingle. Suddenly he felt a little short of breath, like he did when he went up and down the stairs too many times. "Whose?" he asked, but he knew the answer.

"Carlyle's. Found him in the phone book." Randy looked up at Donatto, chuckling as though Angelo were an idiot for asking. "I was there last night *and* the night before. I'll be there every night this week. I want to know where he lives, what the terrain's like, what his habits are." He went back to cleaning the gun. "Why'd you think I wanted to go to the rifle range today?"

Donatto heard a door open down the hall. Angela. She had stayed home from school today. Still in her pajamas and bathrobe, she trudged past them on her way to the kitchen. She stopped when she saw the rifle and the open box of shells. She stared at the weapon, then at Angelo. He almost shrugged an apology—*I know, honey, I know*—but he didn't. Angie was like her mother. She hated the guns.

Without a word, she turned and went into the kitchen.

Donatto waited until he heard her moving around, cabinets opening and closing, water running, before he spoke again. "I can't get messed up in this, Randy," he said quietly. "If anything went wrong—if we were caught—Angie'd be alone."

"And if McConnell spills?" Harvill asked. "The Feds have kept this case alive for thirty years because they're calling the bombing an attempted murder. You wanna be an accessory to that?"

Donatto weighed what his friend was saying. If they killed McConnell now, Angelo could go to jail. However, if they left McConnell alone and someone unmasked him—which those kids seemed ready to do—the singer might tell everything he knew. The FBI would reexamine all the evidence, and Angelo might still go to jail.

He shook his head. It was a lose-lose situation, but he really had only one course. "I'm out," he said. "I'll take my chances defending what I did thirty years ago."

Randy slammed his hand down on the table. "Well, that's not good enough!" he shouted. "I have something to lose here, too!"

Glaring, Angelo stepped toward Randy—not to hit him, but to send a message: Angie was not to hear this conversation. Randy understood. He held up his hands, palms turned out. "Okay, okay," he said.

Angelo heard the microwave humming in the kitchen. "Do whatever you gotta do," he said. "I don't care about McConnell. He can rot in hell. Just leave me out of it."

His friend picked up the rifle and carefully ejected each shell. When he was finished, he placed the shells back in their box and handed the rifle to Donatto. "Fair enough," he said. "I'll use my own gun."

Byte hadn't really believed Ms. Langley was leaving until she passed by the faculty lounge this morning. As she passed, the door swung open and Mrs. Calder, the school secretary, stepped out. She let out a cheery "Whoopsie daisy" as she moved into the corridor, moving aside to avoid bumping into Byte. In one hand, Mrs. Calder held a paper plate bearing a thick slice of pineapple upside-down cake, two chocolate chip cookies, and some kind of rolled up pastry with cream sticking out each end. In the other hand was a plastic fork, and Byte could see traces of pineapple and cake crumbs at the corners of Mrs. Calder's mouth.

Worse, the door to the lounge stood open and Byte could see a table covered with desserts. In the center was a huge greeting card, perhaps a foot and a half tall, covered with scribblings of different sizes and different colors of ink.

A good-bye card signed by the faculty and staff. A good-bye party for Ms. Langley.

The door swung shut, closing off the scene, and Byte felt her eyes burn and her throat tighten.

"It's time we tried to put all this together," Peter said.

Peter, Byte, Jake, and Mattie once again gave up their lunch period to meet in the library. Byte powered up her laptop, but her eyes kept darting over to the elderly woman at the checkout desk. *No doubt the new librarian,* Peter thought. Ms. Langley stood at the woman's shoulder, explaining the CD-ROM system.

"You all right?" Peter asked.

Byte pulled out the photos she had printed last night, setting them on the table and smoothing out the wrinkles with her hand. "I'm *fine,*" she said.

"Jake and I will start," said Mattie. "Last night, we went to the junkyard to look at Josh's van. We showed the mechanic the slashed brake line and asked him if he thought someone might have cut it."

"And?" asked Peter.

"He didn't think so," said Jake.

"I think his exact words," added Mattie, "were 'And who're you? James Bond?'" Mattie then fished around in his pocket and pulled out three small stones. He held them up for Peter to see. Each bore edges that were chipped and ground sharp by passing cars. "Jake and I felt around the underside of the van and found these stuck between the piping. The gravel tore the line, Peter. McConnell and Red Carlyle may be the same person, but he didn't try to kill us that night." With that, Mattie flipped the stones into the air one at a time like coins. He paused, and at the last instant tugged out his shirt pocket to catch them. Peter picked up a hint of triumph in the gesture—Mattie's way of celebrating Red's innocence.

Byte indicated the photos. "Okay, here's Dylan McConnell," she said. "Are he and Red the same guy? We don't know. But here's the interesting thing." She pulled out some other sheets and laid them on the table. "I did some more research—birth records around Toronto, that kind of thing. No one ever heard from Dylan McConnell after April 11, 1970, right? Well, get this. I couldn't find any records on Red Carlyle before August of 1971. It's like Red Carlyle never existed until after McConnell disappeared."

She then turned the second photo around so that Peter and the others could see it. "And look at this."

"*Bonhoffer?*" cried Jake.

"It is him!" said Mattie.

Peter studied the photo and found that he, too, had no doubts. It was FBI agent Paul Bonhoffer. But what did it mean? Perhaps nothing. Bonhoffer could have witnessed the bombing at Trenton State and later dedicated himself to bringing McConnell to justice.

But Bonhoffer had been awfully interested in getting that film. And not just the original, either—he'd wanted every copy.

"We need to look at the film again," Peter said.

Byte slipped her hand into the outer pocket of her computer bag and withdrew a CD. She slid it into the computer's drive, and a moment later Joshua Quinn's image, followed by Dylan McConnell's, played across the screen.

"Peter's dad saw something when the jeeps blew up," Mattie said. "Let's look there." When the moment came, he tapped on the screen. "Now," he said. "Can you slow it down?"

"I can give you frame-by-frame," said Byte.

She keyed in a command, and the screen went from full streaming video to a series of clicking still frames. In super slow motion, the front end of the center jeep rose off the ground an inch, two inches, three inches, and a tiny spray of dirt jetted out from beneath it. The spray grew larger, becoming a cloud—a mixture of dirt from the ground and smoke from the pipe bomb. Peeking out from the center of this cloud was a dot of red-orange flame. The flame also grew larger, expanding until the entire undercarriage of the jeep was aglow. The front end of the jeep, Peter saw, was now easily a foot in the air. The hood slowly lifted, like someone tearing off the lid of a cat food tin. It rose higher, higher, in a series of stop-action jerks, fire fluttering from underneath.

In the next series of frames, the fenders on each side of the jeep broke apart into tiny, razor-sharp puzzle pieces. The pieces flew outward, expanding—*click click click*—until Peter thought they resembled a cloud of angry bees whose hive had been struck to the ground. The pieces of the fender inched toward the other two jeeps, slamming against them. A few ricocheted off; most plowed right through the metal.

At almost the same moment, the tail ends of the other two jeeps rose off the ground. But instead of a cloud of dirt and gas, Peter saw only flames. They erupted from the side of the jeeps, first in a tiny spray, then as a fountain, then as a fireball that spread underneath the jeeps, lifting them even higher. The fireballs rose upward, growing like balloons slowly filling with air. They spread out until they met at the top of the screen—*click click click*—and drifted out of view.

Jake was shaking his head. "I'm no expert, Peter," he said, "but if you ask me, I didn't see any bombs under those other two jeeps. It looked to me like their gas tanks exploded when the first jeep went up."

Peter frowned. "That's wrong. The report at the time said *three* bombs."

And the report had to be right…*right?* Peter tended to view investigative reports as pure fact, with no space for argument. Facts were like the concrete slab underneath a house. You build your case on them.

"Would that be the report written up by National Guardsman Paul Bonhoffer?" asked Mattie.

Of course. Mattie was right. Peter reached over and punched the eject button on Byte's CD-ROM drive. The disk kicked out, and he lifted it from the tray. "Can I take these photos home?" he asked. "I want to show them to my dad—without Bonhoffer hanging around."

"You'll have to admit that we lied about having another copy," said Mattie.

"I didn't lie," said Peter. "Byte did."

Byte handed him the jewel case, refusing to comment.

"One more thing," Peter said. "I think we've gone as far as we can go with this. The only way we're going to find out if Red Carlyle is Dylan McConnell is if we ask him. We'll have to confront him, come right out and tell him we know who he is, and make him admit it."

"He'll just deny it," said Byte.

Peter took the photos and the reports Byte had printed. Smiling, he slipped them into his backpack.

"I think I know a way to make it hard for him to do that," he said.

ten

Thursday evening

mattie wasn't afraid. He glanced over his shoulder at his friends and knocked on Red Carlyle's door. A porch light came on, bathing the front of the house in a yellowish glow. Now Mattie heard footsteps shuffling toward the door.

The door swung open only about four inches and stopped. A shoulder-high brass chain stretched taut between the door and the frame. A portion of a face—one eye, a section of nose, a bit of bearded chin—peered at him through the narrow opening. The rest of the face was in shadow.

"Yeah?"

"Red," said Mattie, "we need to talk."

Randy Harvill sat up a little straighter in the seat of his rental car, a giant Ford Expedition. When a tiny car turned onto the street, Randy reached for his binoculars.

The Volkswagen pulled into Carlyle's driveway. *McConnell's driveway,* he reminded himself. He saw four teenagers get out of the car and walk to the porch. A yellow lamp above the door flicked on, and a moment later, Carlyle let them in.

Randy grunted. One of the kids was huge, well over six feet tall, and had closely cropped blond hair. If killing McConnell meant getting close, he would have to watch that one. Another kid had dark hair and wore glasses with large, round frames that made him look like an owl. Harvill nodded to himself, clicked on a penlight, and fished in his pocket for the business card: Misfits, Inc. Investigations. The names leaped out at him: Jake Armstrong and Peter Braddock. Randy had made Angelo describe the two teenagers who had asked about McConnell. Still, his insides tingled and went cold when he saw them here at McConnell's. He struggled to understand. They were blackmailing McConnell? Demanding money from him, threatening to turn him in? Harvill discarded those ideas. McConnell had all but welcomed them in.

That left only one option. The kids knew the truth. Randy would have to deal with all of them. McConnell, of course, would have to go, but the kids—well, maybe it would be enough to scare them.

The house sat in a quiet neighborhood, one in a group of seven or eight houses on a narrow street, beyond which a ridge of dry grass swept up to a slightly higher elevation. On that flattened hill the community had built its elementary school. Randy had parked the Expedition in the school lot. He'd found a space near the playing field where the pools of light cast by halogen lamps didn't quite overlap, a shadowy area where the Expedition would blend into the darkness. For the last several evenings Randy had come here to watch McConnell and note the singer's comings and goings. But tonight was the first night he'd brought the package with him.

He reached for the bundle he'd stashed on the floor behind his seat. It was over four feet long, and wrapped in a blanket. He held it across his lap, staring through the window at the house.

Randy frowned, reaching again for the binoculars. The porch was dark, but Harvill had seen movement. Someone else had slipped out of the car in the driveway and was walking slowly toward the house. The figure—Randy saw nothing but a vague shape and a moving shadow—crept to the door and opened it.

When the figure vanished into the house, Randy unwrapped his package. The hunting rifle was the Winchester 30.06 his father had given him on his fourteenth birthday. Over the years the wooden grip had almost molded itself to the curve of his hand. *Five hundred yards to McConnell's door,* he'd calculated. He couldn't risk moving in closer—too many houses nearby with lights in the windows. It was a challenging shot even for him, but at that distance, and in the still night air, he would make it.

Randy raised the rifle, pointing it through the open window and staring through the telescopic sight. He imagined Dylan McConnell standing beneath the porch lamp, awash in its sickly glow. As if responding to the image, his finger wrapped around the trigger without squeezing, and his mind filled with one thought.

Boom.

Peter thought it best to start with the accusation.

Red Carlyle led them to his studio and sat on a wooden stool. The Misfits stood in a semicircle facing him. Jake took a tiny Superball from his pocket and let his eyes follow it as it fell to the floor, swallowing it in his palm as it bounced back up. Byte waited silently, studying McConnell, her arms wrapped around her middle. No one spoke. The words had to come from Mattie first, Peter had told them. Red knew Mattie from a couple of lessons now. Mattie was the smallest of the group, the least threatening. Spoken in Mattie's soft voice, the words would slam into Red like a rifle shot. Sensing the moment had come, Peter cocked his head just enough for his friend to see. *Now.*

Mattie sniffled, running a finger along the underside of his nose. "Red," he said, "we know who you are."

Red shrugged and waited for Mattie to explain. Peter could see the tension in Red's muscles. The man sat with his shoulders hunched and his arms loosely crossed, but the looseness looked forced. His eyes darted from one

Misfit to another, trying to gather what it was they thought they knew.

And he looked afraid.

"Thirty years ago," Mattie went on. "Trenton State University. You were the singer on stage. You're Dylan McConnell." He said the words perfectly, Peter thought. His tone was flat, even, quiet. Red, if he were McConnell, would not hear any threat, would not sense anything to make him lash out.

Red glanced at the window, flicking his head in that direction as though considering, for just an instant, escaping through it. "I don't know what you're talking about," he said.

Byte stepped forward. She held a manila folder that contained the materials she had collected. "Red," she said, "hear us out. You don't have to be afraid of us."

She went on to explain what the Misfits had learned—that Red Carlyle did not exist until after Dylan McConnell had vanished, how a film suggested there had been one bomb when the reports claimed three. Red listened, his eyes widening at the mention of the single bomb. Then, just as quickly, his expression hardened.

"I think you all should leave now," he said.

"You know," said Peter, "on the way here, we stopped at a guitar shop. I brought a picture from that day." Byte handed Peter the file folder and he slipped an 8x10 print from it. The image was a single frame from the film Luna had shot, enlarged on Byte's computer. It showed Dylan McConnell holding his small guitar, sunlight glinting off the mother-of pearl inlay around the body and sound hole. "The shop owner identified it as a Martin 00-45," Peter went on. "He said it was an unusual instrument, worth a lot of money. A person who owned a guitar like that, he said, would likely want to keep it…" Peter surveyed the room, studying the guitars.

While Peter spoke, Red had made his way casually toward the worktable, nodding as though he was considering what Peter was saying. Now he moved like lightning, snatching up a loose guitar neck of solid mahogany. He brandished it, and for a moment Peter thought he was going swing it at them. His eyes were wild, and his breathing was scratchy and uneven. The chunk of wood wavered in the air for several seconds, as though deciding for itself what it wanted to do. Then Red collapsed against the table and the guitar neck clattered to the floor. The man's eyes began filling with tears. "Go away," he said, his voice a husky whisper. "Leave me alone."

"Before we do," said Byte, "someone wants to meet you."

The guitar player slipped to his knees, his breath still ragged and his body wracked with a series of coughs. A shadow appeared in the open doorway, and Peter watched as Red's eyes locked on it.

"Dylan McConnell," said Byte's uncle, "my name is Joshua Quinn." Josh pulled up his pant leg, revealing his prosthetic limb.

Red stared at the artificial leg. It seemed to Peter that everything else in the room had vanished. Nothing remained except for that line where Josh's leg ended and a chunk of plastic began. Red sagged, then shifted on the floor so that his back rested against the wall and his knees were drawn up. For a long time the room was silent. Then, in words that were barely discernible, Peter heard Red speak.

"I knew you'd find me," he said.

"So it's true," Peter said. "You *are* Dylan McConnell."

Red nodded.

Peter was surprised when Mattie dropped to the floor and sat next to the man. He seemed perfectly at ease around Red—Dylan—while Peter was still shaking. "Red," Mattie asked, "what really happened back then? Did you set the bomb?"

Red closed his eyes, and rubbed his temples. Peter felt a rush of sympathy for the man. For thirty years he had been Red Carlyle; now someone was asking him to be Dylan McConnell again.

"Yes," McConnell said, "I set the bomb." He looked again at Byte's uncle, and Peter thought the lines around McConnell's eyes deepened. "It wasn't supposed to hurt anyone. It was like…well, like burning down an ROTC building that was going to be demolished anyway. A statement."

Peter thought Josh would say something, but he remained silent, his eyes dark.

"Who'd have known the crowd would move…*forward* like that?" McConnell went on. He paused and reached out in front of him as though grabbing for something. It seemed that the simplest words were escaping him, and McConnell had to reach out and snatch them before they were gone. Finally he gave up, burying his face against his knees. "It was just supposed to be a jeep," he cried, "a single, stupid, rusted-out jeep."

"Only one bomb?" Peter asked.

McConnell looked up and nodded.

"The report," Peter went on, "said three."

"I can't explain that," said McConnell.

Peter, his nerves no longer tingling, risked moving a step closer to the singer. "I can," he said. "Someone lied."

He handed the file folder back to Byte, and each of the Misfits sat on the floor by the singer. Red looked up now, really facing Josh for the first time. Byte's uncle remained standing, unmoved, the overhead lamp throwing a cone of light down across his back and casting a shadow over the group.

"So after the explosion," Peter said, "when you learned that Josh here had lost his leg, you went into hiding."

McConnell nodded. "I hid for two days," he admitted. "Then Monday, when those four students were shot, I realized I had done something terribly wrong. I kept thinking maybe...maybe...if I hadn't destroyed that jeep, the National Guard wouldn't have been so angry. If I hadn't injured your friend here, maybe the protesters wouldn't have been so riled up. Maybe none of it would have happened. Maybe those four students who were killed would be alive today. They'd be parents, or grandparents."

"So you fled to Canada," Byte said.

"A lot of young men did," said McConnell. "They did it because they hated the war. Guess I was the only one who did it because I was a criminal."

"And that's where you met Melanie," said Jake.

McConnell's head swung around, and his eyes locked on Jake. Peter saw a momentary flash of anger pass across the singer's face. McConnell then turned to Mattie, who looked at the floor, his face turning bright red. "Yes."

"And you became Red Carlyle," said Peter.

McConnell nodded.

Byte handed the singer the photo of the National Guardsman. "Do you know this man?" she asked. "His name is Paul Bonhoffer."

McConnell gazed at the photo, then shook his head and handed it back.

"How about an Angelo Donatto?" asked Peter, showing McConnell another photograph.

Again he shook his head.

Peter frowned. "We're missing something, then. We know the original report said there were three bombs, but we don't know why."

"Maybe they were just bad investigators," Jake suggested. "Or just lazy."

"Not likely," said Uncle Josh. "Bombs leave specific traces—chemicals, shrapnel, and the like. A bad investigation might *miss* those things, but there's no way an investigator would say that stuff was there if it wasn't."

The Misfits all looked at Josh. This was the first time he had spoken since introducing himself.

"So if you set only one bomb," said Peter, after a pause, "that means someone else set the other two." He frowned. "Or rigged the investigation."

Peter pondered these new facts. McConnell was already guilty of a crime. Why go to the trouble to make him appear guiltier? Maybe it was personal. Did that make sense? *No*, Peter thought. McConnell didn't recognize Bonhoffer or Donatto.

He shook his head. The Misfits had done what they had set out to do. They had learned that no one had tried to kill them, and they had proven that Red Carlyle and Dylan McConnell were the same man. Their interest in this case had ended.

And yet, Peter thought, he hated to drop it with questions still hanging. Unanswered questions sat in his stomach like rocks. Maybe it wouldn't hurt to clear some of those rocks away.

"We've hit a wall," he said to the others, "but maybe my dad can help us."

They stood up. Mattie reached down to help McConnell to his feet and almost lost his balance. Josh and McConnell looked at each other, and the Misfits found themselves stepping back, giving the men room. *Room for what, though?* Peter wondered. Josh rubbed his hands against his jeans, and Peter thought for a moment that he might take a swing at McConnell. McConnell must have sensed it too. He didn't move, as though expecting, even welcoming the punch.

Instead, Josh stuck out his hand, palm open.

For a moment McConnell did nothing. He just eyed

the hand, reached for it like it might be hot, or sharp, then encircled it with his own delicate, musician's fingers. Peter saw McConnell's eyes moisten. Josh must have seen it too, because he yanked on the arm, drawing McConnell into a powerful bear hug. His hand clapped on McConnell's back, and the singer's body began to shake.

"It's all right," Josh said. "It's all right."

McConnell just whispered the same words over and over. "I'm sorry I'm sorry I'm sorry I'm sorry…"

It was getting late. Byte slung her computer bag over her shoulder. Mattie wanted to show everyone the chords he had learned, so McConnell grabbed a guitar that hung from a padded hook and handed it to him. The guitar was small, Byte noticed, and it had mother-of-pearl inlay around the body and sound hole. The logo on the headstock was in swirling, nineteenth-century letters: C.F. Martin. It was the 00-45 Dylan McConnell had played at Trenton State. Byte wondered how long it would take before Mattie realized what he was holding.

The answer was: not long.

Mattie examined the guitar in his lap. His mouth opened, closed, opened…. Byte laughed. But then, as she looked at him, Mattie almost reminded her of Red Carlyle sitting in the restaurant, singing his stories, or Dylan McConnell in his flag shirt, singing to end a war.

Byte's heart began to pound. *Singing to end a war.*

She looked at the old singer, an idea playing at the edges of her mind. She wasn't thinking so much about ending a war as about starting one. "Mr. McConnell," she asked, crinkling her nose to set her glasses straight, "how would you feel about going into battle again?"

They're leaving.

When McConnell's porch light came on again, Randy reached for the Winchester once more. He'd have no better opportunity.

This time McConnell walked outside with his visitors rather than hiding behind the door. The kids, joined by a man Randy didn't recognize, walked to the car in the driveway. Randy snorted. The kids were *waving* at McConnell. The girl even hobbled back on her crutches and threw one arm around McConnell's neck.

No blackmail there.

Randy chambered the first shell. McConnell must not be allowed to tell his story.

Five hundred yards. A still night. A bright porch lamp.

Randy stared down the sight, held his breath, and squeezed the trigger.

Peter heard a sound like a firecracker. At almost the same instant, the frame of McConnell's front door—just inches from the singer's head—exploded into a shower of wood splinters. McConnell frowned, reaching toward the jagged tear to find out what had caused it. Before he touched it, though, another firecracker sounded, and Peter watched in horror as McConnell spun around and slammed into the door. The singer slipped to the ground, a red spot blossoming across his chest.

Byte shrieked.

Pop! Josh's leg flew out from under him, and he fell into the dark bushes next to the porch.

Pop! The asphalt at Peter's feet spit up around his ankles. A moment later, something plowed into his stomach, knocking the breath from him and driving him to the ground. He looked up to see Jake leaning over him. Jake grabbed Peter's legs and dragged him so that both boys lay behind the front end of Jake's car.

Pop! One of Byte's crutches spiraled out of her hand as though kicked. It clattered across the driveway, out of reach. She gazed down at her hand, and Peter could see blood dripping from it. She dropped the other crutch and dove to the ground, hauling herself across the asphalt until she, too, lay hidden behind Jake's Escort.

Seeing Byte's hand, Jake looked down at his denim jacket, then at Peter's long-sleeved T-shirt. "Sorry," he said. He gripped Peter's shirt where sleeve met the shoulder and tore it off at the seam. "Here," he said. He took Byte's wounded hand and bound it in the fabric, making a temporary bandage.

"Where's Josh?" Byte asked.

Peter looked back at the doorway. Josh was lost in the shadows. McConnell, however, still lay where he had fallen. Peter could see his chest rising and falling, but the man's breathing appeared fast and shallow. "We've got to get him out of there," Peter said. "He's dead if we don't." Peter heard the popping again, and a hole punched through McConnell's front door, just above the singer's right shoulder.

"What do you want to do?" asked Jake.

Good question, Peter thought. They were pinned behind the car, with no way to move until the shooting stopped. Unless they wanted to be shot themselves, they would just have to sit there and wait. What were their options? The shooter must be using a rifle. How much ammunition would he have? How soon before the man—or woman—would have to reload? Even a short pause would give Peter and Jake the few seconds they would need to drag McConnell to safety.

Peter looked at the porch again. Stunned, he watched as McConnell's limp body began to slide into the house all by itself. First his head went, then his shoulders, chest, legs, feet—all vanishing in a series of slow jerks. Within minutes, Peter heard the sound of sirens wailing in the distance.

attie, it turned out, had sneaked to the rear of McConnell's house when the shooting started. He had slipped in through a window, made his way to the door, and dragged McConnell in by the arms. Once inside, he had pressed a towel to McConnell's wound and called 911.

Now police swarmed the house and the nearby school. One uniformed officer—a baby-faced young man who looked fresh from the academy, Peter thought—used a knife to dig a rifle bullet from the door frame. He found another in the ceiling of McConnell's entryway. It had struck the concrete porch and ricocheted upward into the house.

After answering a million questions, the Misfits and Josh raced to the hospital to check on McConnell. There, an emergency room surgeon was removing a bullet from McConnell's chest—just above the right lung and below the collarbone. The nurse told Peter that the surgeon would just have to clean the wound, suture it up, and

chapter eleven

bandage it. McConnell would spend the night in the hospital and go home tomorrow. When she finished, she looked at each of the Misfits and Josh, clearly remembering them from the car accident. "Hmph," she said. "We ought to start handing out those cards like they do at the frozen yogurt shop. Buy twelve, get one free." She stormed back behind the desk and rifled through a stack of forms, grumbling as she did.

"Could have been a lot worse," Jake said to the others.

Peter nodded. He had thought Josh was shot, but a bullet had only grazed his artificial leg, sending it spinning out from under him.

The door to the emergency room burst open, and Byte's mom rushed in. She glowered at the other Misfits just before she examined Byte's bandaged hand. The doctor had given Byte seven stitches in the web of skin between her thumb and index finger. Mrs. Salzmann whispered something to her daughter, then drew her into a tight hug. She studied the doctor's handiwork, kissed Byte on the cheek, and went over to talk to Josh.

Peter sidled over to Byte. "What did she say?" he asked.

Byte flushed. "She said that Misfits, Inc. had better start offering medical insurance."

With that, Peter decided he'd better keep Byte out of trouble for a while.

He gestured for Jake and Mattie. The group huddled together, away from Josh and Byte's mom.

"I think it's best to let the police handle the shooting," Peter said. "At this point, they have more information than we do." He looked at Byte. "I do want that CD-ROM, though," he added, "the one with Luna's film on it. And the file you put together. I think it's time my dad learned something about his new partner, Agent Bonhoffer."

Byte, nodding, reached into her computer bag for the file folder and the jewel box containing the CD-ROM disk. She handed both to Peter.

"What do you think your dad's gonna do?" Mattie asked.

Peter thought a moment, frowning. "I dunno."

Federal Bureau of Investigation,
Bugle Point Office
Friday morning

Nick Braddock thrust open the office door and it slammed against the inside wall. He saw Agent McNab sitting at a desk, fussing with a stack of paperwork and wiping his fingers with a napkin. A half-eaten cheese danish and a cup of cappuccino sat on the desktop next to McNab's computer keyboard. Polaski was on the phone; he spun his chair in Nick's direction when he heard the door slam.

"Where is he?" Nick demanded.

Polaski shrugged.

Nick turned to McNab. "Bonhoffer. Where is he?"

McNab froze, the napkin still pressed against his fingers. His eyes flickered toward the Chief's office. Nick looked through the frosted glass wall and saw two dim figures. Glancing back at Polaski, he stormed toward the office door and, without knocking, thrust it open.

Bonhoffer was sitting calmly in a chair. He looked up at Nick, one eyebrow raised in disapproval.

"The conference room," Nick said. "Now."

Nick guided Bonhoffer through the door of the room and slammed it shut behind them. He dropped his briefcase on the table and opened it, taking out the file and the CD-ROM disk Peter had given him last night. He slid the disk across the table to Bonhoffer.

Neither man sat.

"That disk," Nick said, "contains the Trenton State film. I had our demolitions expert examine frame-by-frame footage of the jeep explosions. He confirms what my son suspected. One bomb, Bonhoffer. Not three." He moved around the table, bringing himself face to face with Bonhoffer's casual smirk. "But you knew that, didn't you?"

Bonhoffer didn't answer, but the smirk flattened into something more…doubtful? Fearful? Nick opened up the file next, taking out the photo of the National Guardsman Byte had printed off from the disk. "You know," said Nick, "when I went through the FBI file on Dylan McConnell, all the stuff you brought with you from Washington, I never found anything that mentioned you were a Guardsman at Trenton State." He thrust the photo against Bonhoffer's chest. Bonhoffer trapped it there with his hands, and the paper crackled.

"Why is that, Paul? Why is it that all the reports are wrong about the number of bombs?" Nick leaned close to the other agent, their noses almost touching. "You've put together a lot of material. The file on April 11, 1970 is about two inches thick. Statements from Guardsmen. Statements from witnesses." Nick's voice grew louder so that he was almost yelling. "So why is it, Paul, that in thirty years, and in all those documents, *I can't find a single sheet of paper with your name on it?* You were there. Why aren't you listed with the other Guardsmen?"

Bonhoffer didn't flinch. He stared at Nick, and his mouth curled into a smile. "That information is on a need-to-know basis," he said. He reached up and straightened the knot in his tie. "And you, Agent Braddock, do *not* need to know."

Nick grabbed the agent by the front of his shirt, crumpling the fabric in his fists. He swung Bonhoffer around and pinned him against the wall. "Someone took a shot at my son last night, Bonhoffer," he growled, "so I *do* need to know. You were at Trenton State. You were in charge of the unit that stormed the crowd that day. I've got the photo to prove it. You also set up a false investigation that claimed there were three bombs when there was only one. I've got the film to prove that. The only thing I don't know, Bonhoffer, is *why.*"

"I wasn't there!" Bonhoffer said.

"You're lying!"

"*I wasn't there!*"

Nick tightened his grip on Bonhoffer's shirt and shook

the man. Bonhoffer looked Nick in the eye, knowing full well the explanation would come here, now, or later in Washington.

His body sagged. "It wasn't me," he said. "It was my brother, Hugh."

Nick, McNab, Polaski, and the Chief sat around the conference table. Bonhoffer faced them, his head in his hands, a cassette recorder on the table in front of him.

"Hugh," he said, "discovered the bomb under the jeep before it went off." He paused, letting the words hang in the air a moment before continuing. "He told some of his troop about it, and they planned to evacuate the area, call out the bomb squad—you know the drill. But these protesters, these anarchists, had been needling the Guardsmen for hours. Shouting at them. Calling them names. Spitting on them." Bonhoffer looked up at the other agents. "Don't you see? The jeep was old—Korean War issue. The Guard would have replaced it soon enough anyway." He picked up a paper clip and began twisting it in his fingers. "So...someone suggested they could just *leave* the bomb there. Let the jeep go. It would give them an excuse to pound a few heads. The crowd was a safe distance away. The explosion wouldn't hurt anyone."

"What were the other jeeps doing right next to it?" Nick asked.

"Coincidence. General Bettencourt's men just happened to park there," Bonhoffer replied. "He didn't know about the bomb, and Hugh couldn't tell him. When it went off, the fuel tanks of the other two jeeps went up as well. I'm pretty sure it was McConnell who set the bomb to begin with. I'm also pretty sure he just intended to destroy some property; he wasn't planning to hurt anyone. Stupid fool—who can control these kinds of things?" The paper clip was a twisted mess. Bonhoffer tossed it to the table, and it skittered off the edge and fell to the carpet.

"So when all three jeeps blew up, McConnell *and* your brother had a whole new problem," the Chief noted.

Bonhoffer nodded. "Hugh learned later that a young man had lost his leg in the explosions. The medical report said that the shrapnel that had injured the man came from a jeep's *fuel tank*. Do you see now?"

"A fuel tank," Nick echoed. "Joshua Quinn wasn't directly injured by the bomb, then. It was one of the other jeeps—the secondary explosions—that cost him his leg."

"Yes," said Bonhoffer. "That injury made it possible for the FBI to call the bombing attempted murder. It's the only thing that's kept the case against Dylan McConnell open after all these years. No one would have pursued the man three decades over a wrecked jeep." Bonhoffer paused and rubbed at his eyes, which had become red rimmed and bloodshot. "But it's even more complicated than that," he said.

Polaski had been taking notes. With these last words, he tossed down his pen and leaned back in his chair. "The massacre," he said.

"Yes."

Nick understood now. By ignoring the bomb, Hugh Bonhoffer had unwittingly played a role in one of the Vietnam War's most painful tragedies. The shootings on April 13, 1970, were a result of human weakness, evil, and old-fashioned arrogance. The three days leading up to April 13 were like the slow, careless building of a wildfire. A protester throwing a rock at a Guardsman—there's your dry tinder. A Guardsman swinging his billy club at a girl's head—there's your spray of gasoline. The situation was just barely under control—unless something came along to ignite it all.

Three exploding jeeps and an amputated leg, Nick thought, *would have made a powerful torch.*

"Hugh never really recovered," Bonhoffer went on. "He'd already served a tour in Vietnam, but after the shootings, he asked to be activated into regular Army duty again. This time he…he never made it home."

"Let me work out the rest," Polaski said. "All these years, you've blamed McConnell for your brother's death. You've made it your life's mission to capture him, to see him behind bars."

Bonhoffer lowered his head again. "No," he whispered. "You've got it wrong. It was all about protecting Hugh. I wanted to bury the case. I never wanted it solved. I never wanted to hear from McConnell again."

An hour later, Nick, McNab, Polaski, the Chief, and eight other agents surrounded the home of one Angelo

Donatto, semiretired construction worker and former National Guardsman. Donatto had been at Trenton State, according to Bonhoffer, and clearly had a motive for wanting McConnell to remain silent. Furthermore, Peter had told Nick about the guns. Donatto was now the prime suspect in last night's shooting at Red Carlyle's house.

Agents huddled at each door and window. A whispered command came through their headsets, and the men at the doors raised steel battering rams. At the next command, they smashed through the doors and swarmed inside the house with weapons raised.

"Federal agents! Get down!" they shouted. "Get down!" The words echoed over and over.

A teenaged girl screamed and cowered to the floor. Donatto himself looked like he might resist, but he saw the guns, saw his daughter's terror, and his hands went behind his head. Polaski cuffed him and took him away while a female agent calmed the girl.

It took three days to do ballistics tests on all of Donatto's guns. The man owned almost three dozen, and each had to be fired, the spent bullets compared to the one taken from Red Carlyle's chest. Since that bit of evidence sat in the hands of the Bugle Point PD, the FBI scientists would have to work with police scientist Marco Weese in order to finish the work. Three days. When Nick finally heard the results, he fumed.

All of Donatto's guns were licensed.

All of the guns were accounted for.

None of the guns matched the one that had been used to shoot Red Carlyle.

And so, the Chief told Nick, there was nothing left for them to do. With apologies, the FBI sent Donatto home.

chapter twelve

Two weeks later

byte unfurled the banner she had painted and held one corner of it to the cafeteria wall. She slapped down a strip of masking tape to hold one side, but had to let the banner dangle a few seconds while she struggled on her crutches to reach the other corner. Once there, she tore another strip from the roll and taped that end of the banner to the wall. When finished, she shuffled back a few steps to admire her work.

It's beautiful, she thought.

At first, Byte believed the sign should read Volunteer Sign-up for Protest Concert. Then she'd decided the shorter Concert Sign-up might be better, or Save Ms. Langley. But Peter had pointed out that Mr. Steadham would definitely stop them if he knew what they were doing; he suggested something vaguer would work just as well and attract less attention from the principal. He'd been right.

The banner was a work of art—one word in huge balloon letters, surrounded by a psychedelic swirl of colors.

Here, it said, followed by an arrow pointing downward.

Red Carlyle had already applied for city permits so that they could hold the concert on the beach. Everything else, he'd told the Misfits, was up to them. Byte had arranged for three of the hottest local rock band to perform. Now she needed help: people to donate lumber and tools, people to construct a small, temporary stage, people to rent and operate lighting equipment, people to move through the crowd with petitions, people to pass out buttons saying Scare Your Parents—Read a Book! Mostly, they needed people to come and watch—and attend the school board meeting scheduled for the day after the concert. Byte and Peter planned to sit beneath this banner during lunch every day this week, signing up volunteers.

Byte had also called Rebecca Kaidanov at the *Bugle Point Courier* to ask for help, and boy, did Rebecca come through! Yesterday the front-page story in the newspaper's Metro section was all about the concert. A large photo splashed across the middle of the page showed Ms. Langley with the four Misfits, their arms around one another's shoulders and their bare feet dug into the beach sand where, in two weeks, the concert would happen.

Peter set up a card table and unfolded two metal chairs. "Where's Mattie?" Byte asked.

"Working the room," said Peter.

Of course. Next to the cheerleaders selling their candygrams, she and Peter looked like any other student club running a fundraiser. They blended in so well, in fact, that Mattie was conducting a massive word-of-mouth campaign to let students know what they were doing, starting this morning with a chain-letter note in first period. Now he was wandering the lunchroom, pointing students toward the banner.

Byte saw a figure approaching and cringed. It was Toby Atherton, the basketball player Byte's uncle had humiliated. He walked up to the table, his shoulders hunched and his hands stuffed into the pockets of his letterman's jacket. "Hey, computer chick," he said. Byte said nothing, but she reached for her computer bag, her arms wrapping around it instinctively. Peter stared at Atherton and set down his sign-up sheet and a stack of fliers. Byte could feel his body tense. *Please,* she thought, *not another fight. Not here. Not now.*

Atherton dug into his hip pocket for a pen. He held it up and clicked it. "So," he said, "you got a petition going or something?"

Byte swallowed, then nodded.

Atherton turned and gazed across the room, looking for someone. He waved at a table, seeking that person's attention, and then he nodded as if to say *Yeah. Over here.*

A moment later Byte counted five—no, six—members of the JV basketball team heading across the lunchroom. A moment later they clustered around Peter and Byte. Atherton had already signed the petition. Now he was adding his name to the volunteer list as well. "Gonna be hot at the beach," he said flatly, and then, after his name, he scribbled down his pledge to bring six cases of bottled water.

Byte didn't know what to say, so she just said, "Thank you."

Beyond the group of basketball players, she saw several more students rise and begin walking in her direction. She looked at Peter. *Can you believe this?* He smiled but said nothing.

One of the students gazed down at the stack of fliers, clearly impressed by the list of bands. "So who's the 'Special Mystery Guest'?" he asked.

"If we told you," said Peter, "it wouldn't be a mystery."

The kid laughed and scribbled down his name.

When the student wandered off, Peter leaned over and whispered to Byte. "Is our 'guest' going to perform as Red Carlyle," he asked, "or as Dylan McConnell?"

Byte shrugged. "I don't think he's made up his mind yet." She reached over and squeezed Peter's hand. "What about you?" she asked. "Have you told your dad? I mean, that McConnell and Carlyle are the same person?"

Peter shook his head. "No."

Byte understood. She wouldn't have said anything either.

The crowd around their table began to thicken again. As students signed their names, Byte tried to peer past them into the lunchroom. "Hey," she said, "where do you suppose Jake went?"

On the far side of the lunchroom, two pay phones hung on the wall near a bank of snack and soda machines. A sophomore girl in a tight pink sweater jabbered away on one phone, whining to her mom about how bad her migraine was…and couldn't her mom come pick her up early 'cause she was *sick*…and would it be all right to stop at the mall on the way home and take another look at that Hilfiger outfit?

No one was using the other phone at the moment. Jake rustled the slip of paper in his pocket. He dug it out and stared at it. It was small and wrinkled and torn along one edge, but in the middle, written in Jake's hasty scrawl, was Angie Donatto's phone number.

He pictured her now in his mind. In the last few days, when he'd had a little more time to think, he was surprised to find that he often thought of her. She was sick with something, that was obvious, but she also seemed tough and a little smart-alecky. For some reason, Jake found those qualities appealing.

He dug into his pocket again, this time for loose change.

While he fed in the change and dialed the number, he forced himself to stare out over the cafeteria instead of hunching anxiously over the phone. The number rang three times. It had started to ring a fourth time—Jake came very close to hanging up—when a girl's voice answered. "Hello?"

Without his willing them to, Jake's shoulders suddenly straightened. "Hello," he said, "is this Angela?"

"Yeah. Who is this?"

"It's Jake. Jake Armstrong. I came over…to talk to your dad. I'm the tall guy, remember? Blond hair? I was just thinking—"

"*Hiiiiiii*," she said. The word went up in pitch then dropped back down, like a blues note.

"You stayed home from school," Jake said. "I guess that means you're not feeling well, huh?"

A long pause. "Either that," she admitted, "or it's a convenient excuse. Did you know Dave Matthews was on *The View* today?"

Jake laughed, and for the next ten minutes the two talked about music. He tried to explain why he liked Charlie Parker but hated Thelonius Monk. She argued that the Beatles' *Rubber Soul* was really a much better album than *Sgt. Pepper's Lonely Hearts Club Band*. Jake confessed that be-bop improvisation, as difficult as it was, was his favorite jazz form. Angela told him that modern country music was really pop, and modern bluegrass was really country.

"So what's pop, then?" Jake asked.

"Pop," she replied, "is Barbra Streisand on one end and Britney Spears on the other. I shudder to go there."

Jake laughed. He *liked* this girl. "Well, let me ask you this," he said. "How do you feel about folk music?"

He told her about the book banning at school, about Ms. Langley's resignation, and about the concert on the beach. Angela listened and asked lots of pointed questions. He wasn't exactly thrilled at the idea of running

180 into her dad again, so he asked if she'd like to meet him there.

She said, "Absolutely."

"You gonna ask your dad for permission?" Jake asked.

Now it was her turn to laugh. "I'll leave him a note."

Dylan McConnell stared at the telephone.

Strange, he thought, how quickly he had started thinking of himself as Dylan McConnell again. After thirty years of being Red Carlyle, he would have guessed that the fake name would have become all too real—like any lie when it's told so often and so many people believe it. But once those kids confronted him with the truth—and Red no longer had the strength to deny it—he began to sense just how shallow his fakery was. He tried—he really tried—to think of himself as Red Carlyle. Life would be so much easier if he could maintain that pose. But even saying the name now felt like putting on a dime store Halloween mask; it was a plastic face digging into his own real skin.

The picture in the paper of the kids and the librarian looked great, he thought. The woman who had written up the article in the *Courier*—what was her name? Kaidanov?—had really played up the concert, tantalizing readers with the idea of a "mystery guest."

And who would this mystery guest be, he wondered. Red Carlyle, or Dylan McConnell? If he performed as Red, the audience would leave with a smile, but the smile would fade by the following morning as each person struggled with the demands of a new day. Red Carlyle was too much of an unknown to reach much deeper. Yet if he performed as Dylan McConnell, the media would swarm all over the concert. Newspaper, radio, and television news teams would broadcast his name even as he stepped on stage. The FBI would no doubt be there as well. They would wait at the sidelines, letting him finish his set, and then they would present him with their thirty-year-old arrest warrant. The broadcast reporters would call to him for a comment as he passed by them in handcuffs. A million people would see him on the morning news. The kids' message would get across. He reached for the phone now. He couldn't really choose between the two names. The plastic mask no longer fit. Drawing in a deep breath, he dialed the number for the *Courier*. When the switchboard answered, he asked to speak to Rebecca Kaidanov.

"Features, Kaidanov," said a woman's voice. Her accent was faintly Russian.

"Hello," said McConnell, taking a deep breath. "My name is Dylan McConnell. I think you're going to want to talk to me…."

He told her everything—who he was, why he was calling, when she could interview him. When he was finished, he reached for the old Martin 00-45 that hung from its hook on the wall. A spray bottle containing guitar polish sat on his workbench. He stared at the blackened nicks and dings on the guitar's surface, reached for a cloth, and wondered just how much of the dirt he could rub off.

The Vietnam Veterans Memorial
National Mall, Washington D.C.

Funny, Paul Bonhoffer thought. *They were right all along.*

The sun shone bright and hot across his back, and Paul retreated into the shade cast by the Wall's great sheets of granite. He did not carry his briefcase with him. He did not think of work—or of Dylan McConnell. His file on McConnell was now with Special Agent Braddock in the Bugle Point field office. Nor did he wander around the memorial, as he so liked to do. No, today Bonhoffer walked in a straight line toward the Wall's apex, where he would find his brother's name.

On his way he passed a man in a wheelchair whose legs were both severed at the knees, the stumps wrapped in flesh-colored bandages. The man touched a name on the Wall, weeping. As Paul passed, he laid his hand on the man's shoulder.

A few steps later he stood where the east and west wall met, staring at his brother's name.

Hugh, he told him, *it's over.* Braddock would take over the investigation now, of course. Braddock would be the one to uncover whether Red Carlyle and Dylan McConnell were the same man. *He's a good agent, Hugh,*

Paul added. *When he learns the truth, he'll do the right thing.*

Whatever that might be.

Paul reached into his coat pocket and took out an old wooden top, a toy that had belonged to Hugh when they were children. He had dug it out of a box in his parents' basement. The red paint was chipped; the steel tip was ragged and blunt. On the upper part of it were several tiny holes, which made the top whistle when it spun. Along the side were the words Duncan Whistler. Paul smiled as he remembered his ten-year-old brother on the sidewalk outside their house, his fingers wrapping a string around the top, then flicking it toward the ground. The string unwound, the top hit the ground spinning, and the whistling began. Watching it skitter along, the two boys laughed until it finally wobbled and fell over.

Paul gazed down at the top, ran his finger over it, and set it at the base of the Wall under his brother's name. He then reached out his hand, touching the letters on the Wall itself. He felt a searing in his eyes, and tears began to roll down his cheeks.

Yes, they were right all along, he thought. *Everyone weeps at the Wall.*

Friday
Bugle Point Pier

n ervous?" asked Jake. "I mean, this *is* our party."
"Hunh uh," said Byte, wringing her hands.

"Not in the least," replied Peter, cracking his knuckles.
Peter never cracked his knuckles.

From the Misfits' vantage point near the stage, Jake
looked out over the beach. The band—three guys, with
a girl who had spiked green hair on bass—sounded all
right, but Jake was more interested in the crowd. He had
not seen Angie yet. She wouldn't just stand him up, he
knew, but what if she had gotten sick? He had told her
where to meet him, but what if she couldn't find him?

He turned back to the stage. The last of the opening
acts, a group called Turbulence, was just finishing, the
lead singer dropping to his knees and running his fingers through the thick curly hair that fell across his face.
Jake thought the guy was exactly like Eddie Vedder of
Pearl Jam…only without the talent and intensity.

Where was Angie?

A crowd of perhaps four hundred people—students from BPHS and other high schools, college kids who had seen the newspaper story, adults interested in the book-banning—applauded as the band hammered out a final power chord and took a bow.

Jake felt a tug on his jacket. A voice said, "Sorry I'm late. Never trust a bald chick, huh?"

He spun around, and there stood Angie Donatto. She wore boots, a pair of jeans with a hole in one knee, a tie-dyed T-shirt, and a leather jacket that hung past her hips. A baseball cap sat backwards on her head.

Jake grinned. For some reason he didn't understand, he was glad she hadn't worn the wig. "Hey there," he said. He put an arm around her, a hug for hello.

"Hey yourself," she said.

Jake heard a throat clearing sound behind him. When he turned, he found Byte staring at him, a strange, closed-mouth smile on her face. "I'm Byte," she said, extending her hand to Angie. "Jake didn't say he'd invited anyone."

They shook hands. "I'm Angie Donatto. Nice to meet you."

Jake, red-faced, stepped in to finish the introductions.

As he did, a tiny figure leaped onto the stage, striding to a microphone. It was Mattie, and he moved with the quickness and ease of a *Tonight Show* comic. Maybe it was the energy of the crowd, or maybe the presence of the news teams, or maybe it was just the way Rebecca Kaidanov laughed whenever Mattie took the stage, but the little guy had turned into a total ham. Too small to stand behind the mike, Mattie yanked it from the stand and prowled the stage with it.

"How you doing?" he shouted. "You doing all right?"

The crowd screamed.

"All right!" he went on. "Don't forget to sign the petitions going around. E-mail your school board member! Make sure you attend the meeting Monday night at the county board of education office! And remember…" He grasped the large metal button pinned to his shirt, holding it up for everyone to see. "Scare your parents—read a book!"

The crowd screamed again.

"It's time for our featured guest," Mattie continued. "Ladies and gentlemen…the one! The only! Dylan McConnell!"

Several photographers surged forward, their flashes creating a dizzying strobe pattern. Behind the photographers stood Peter's dad. Nick Braddock's arms were folded, and his face had the stern look of an FBI agent at work. Mr. Braddock had been around all evening. Now the agent was focused on the shadows at the rear of the stage, and Jake felt a pang of sorrow for the man waiting back there. McConnell had already promised to turn himself in on Monday. Jake figured Peter's dad wanted to be here tonight to get a look at the singer, to take in some early impressions.

A moment later, Dylan McConnell stepped from the shadows and moved into a pool of light created by two colored spotlights hanging from an aluminum scaffold.

"So, is this guy any good?" asked Angie.
Jake looked at her. "He's the best."

Randy Harvill watched the concert from the confines of
a lifeguard tower several hundred yards down the beach.
The tower was perfect. Its tiny shack hid him from
observers, the cutout window gave him a perfect view of
McConnell through his binoculars, and its location
allowed him quick access to the parking lot and his car. At
his feet lay the Winchester 30.06, wrapped in an oversized
beach towel. He didn't expect to need it. It was an extra
precaution. Plan B. In a shoulder holster, and hidden by a
light windbreaker jacket, was a .38 caliber snub-nosed
revolver. Randy didn't expect to need it either, but its
weight and presence were oddly comforting.

Those kids had been right.

Carlyle and McConnell were the same man. He had
admitted it. The newspaper had reported it. Randy
sighed. *If only McConnell had gone down permanently a
few weeks ago*, he told himself, *life would have been so
much easier.* The trouble Randy had gone to in order to
get that single brick of C4....

He glanced at his watch. 8:37. In twenty-three minutes, at exactly 9:00 P.M., Dylan McConnell—and hope-
fully those four nosy kids—would be nothing more than
body parts scattered across several dozen square yards of
beach.

C4 was a waxlike substance that came in small bricks
wrapped in paper. It looked like sticks of butter you'd

find in the supermarket, the only difference being that C4 was explosive...a good deal more explosive than dynamite. Around 2:00 A.M., Randy had come here to the beach, to the stage structure that had been finished only hours earlier, and had crawled underneath the plywood platform. There, on the underside of the stage itself, he had placed a simple time bomb—a battery-powered digital timer, a detonator, and a single brick of C4.

You live by the bomb, McConnell, Harvill thought, *you die by the bomb.*

Live by the bomb, and you die by the bomb, Randy had said.

Donatto couldn't pay attention to the television as his friend's words echoed in his mind. He had stared when Randy said them, and when his friend reached into a box and took out a rectangular brick wrapped in paper, Donatto had held up his hand to stop him from explaining. He didn't have to know what Randy planned. He didn't want to know.

After raising the volume a bit, Donatto tossed down the remote and went back to staring blankly at the TV screen. The baseball game suddenly made no sense to him. The announcer was a jabbering idiot.

Live by the bomb...

A newspaper lay open on the table in front of him. Those four kids looked up at Donatto, smiling. He recognized two of them—the one in the round glasses and the

big one who had made Angie smile. The other two
Donatto had never seen before, but he knew their names.

Of course, he knew what Randy was planning. The
newspaper article about McConnell, the concert at the
beach, and the brick wrapped in paper told him everything he needed to know. Donatto had a flash—an
image of the wooden stage rising up in a cloud of fire
and toothpick-sized splinters—but then just as quickly
he clamped a lid on the thought. Who cared if
McConnell died? The man had betrayed his country. He
had betrayed the young men his own age who had
fought and died. He was wanted for attempted murder.
Donatto felt no pity for him. If not for Angie, Donatto
would be right out there with his friend, helping him
place the bomb and set the timer.

And if a handful of people, those in the first few rows
from the stage, got hurt—well, they were just casualties
of justice.

Donatto tried to tell himself he really felt that way, but
his stomach still squirmed at the idea.

He suddenly realized he was hungry. Angie had gone
off somewhere, and he'd been alone with his thoughts
most of the afternoon. He hadn't eaten. He pushed himself up from the couch and trudged to the kitchen,
remembering the six-pack and the leftover pizza that
were sitting in the fridge.

That's where he found the note.

It hung on the refrigerator door, held in place by a
rubber magnet in the shape of a butterfly.

Dad,
Went to check out the concert at the beach.
Be back late.
Love,
Angie

Donatto snatched the note off the refrigerator and held it, the paper rattling in his fingers. His insides collapsed into a hard ball in his stomach.

He grabbed his truck keys from the wooden peg beside the door and ran from the house. All he could think about as he gunned the truck's engine and squealed out of his driveway was that Angie loved music. She loved it more than anything.

When the bomb went off, she'd be right up front.

♪

8:37

Randy gazed through his binoculars at the stage. From this distance, McConnell appeared tiny, thin and stoop-shouldered. Randy could hear the singer's voice and guitar coming through the huge stage amplifiers. It sounded soft and gentle and far away, like a radio playing in another room. He let the binoculars dangle from around his neck and reached for the Winchester, cradling it in his lap. Then he glanced at his watch again, surprised at how slow it seemed to be moving.

Eighteen minutes.

8:42

Angie stood on her tiptoes and gave Jake a light peck on the cheek. He looked down at her, his eyes widening for an instant, and then his face turned bright red. Angie laughed. A moment later, that girl, the one Jake called Byte, turned her back and started muttering to the guy with the round glasses.

All right, so kissing Jake was a little bold, Angie thought, but he was cute. She glanced around at the stage and the large crowd. And not only cute—he and his friends had cooked up this show on their own, which meant he had some brains and guts. She let her hand dangle close to his, their fingers brushing, and then his hand swallowed hers up. She closed her eyes and leaned her head against his shoulder.

The singer's voice was sweet and husky, and Angie decided this was the nicest evening she'd spent with anyone in a really long time.

8:44

Donatto swerved into the beach parking lot. The truck fishtailed, its rear end screeching as it swung out and slammed into the concrete base of a light pole. He gunned the engine again, and the truck shot forward.

When it finally stopped, it sat diagonally behind two parked cars.

He leaped out, slamming the door behind him. In the distance, someone was singing a song Donatto remembered from high school. The only music behind the voice was a clean, fingerpicked guitar.

McConnell.

Donatto ran toward the sound. His heart pounded in his chest, and he only hoped he could find Angie before it stopped beating entirely. He felt stiff and awkward running. And slow—way too slow. *Too much pizza. Too much beer. Old fool,* his mind screamed, *you should have stayed in better shape.* The problem only got worse when he hit the sand. The grainy powder sucked at his shoes with every step. It worked its way through the fabric of his socks and scraped at his ankles. He slipped and fell once and had to haul himself to his feet, spitting sand from his mouth.

He could see the crowd now, hundreds of people sitting picnic style on the beach. A little farther was the stage, and McConnell stood there singing, lit in the glare of a couple of spotlights. *Your fault,* Donatto thought. *All your fault.* He moved swiftly along the edge of the crowd, his eyes scanning each row for his daughter. In the darkness, it seemed she could be almost anyone. Donatto felt a rush of panic when he realized he didn't know if she had worn her wig tonight. He tore through a section of the audience, kicked over someone's soft drink, and clutched at the shoulder of a long-haired brunette in a beret. She turned toward him. It wasn't

Angie. A moment later he grabbed another person's arm, only to find he'd approached a slender young boy who had shaved his hair down to nothing.

Donatto continued moving. *The front,* he reminded himself. *She'd want to be up front.*

He saw her in the first row. With her back turned, she could have been anyone, but she was wearing her Fender ball cap and his leather bomber jacket. Donatto recognized the way the wrinkled collar stood on end and the way the jacket draped so ridiculously on his daughter's tiny frame. He also recognized the tall, muscular boy standing next to her. He was one of the boys who had asked about McConnell, the one that had made Angie smile. Angie was holding his hand, leaning against him, the two swaying in rhythm with the music.

As he rushed toward her, Donatto suddenly realized that he hadn't seen her look that happy in a very long time.

8:51

"Hey, Byte," said Mattie, "this is great." His eyes scanned the huge crowd and makeshift stage. "We ought to do it again next month."

Peter winced. He knew what was coming. Byte popped Mattie on the head with her stack of petitions.

"Okay, okay," said Mattie, laughing. "I know it was a lot of work, but it's fun, right? I mean, look at Jake. He's definitely having a good time."

Byte smacked him again, a lot harder this time. Peter decided that it might be a good idea for Mattie to keep his opinions to himself for a while.

Peter had been paying attention to the music, but now he caught a sudden movement out of the corner of his eye. A shadow loomed closer, growing larger until it stepped into the spill of light from the stage. Peter saw a thickly built man with short salt-and-pepper hair. The man's chest was heaving, and though the evening was pleasantly cool, sweat poured down his face. A moment passed before Peter recognized the man as Angelo Donatto. Donatto moved toward the girl, Angie, and his fingers wrapped around her upper arm. Peter heard her shriek as though someone had awakened her from a dream.

"Dad?" she cried.

Donatto's grip on her tightened, and he tugged her to her feet. "You're coming home," he said. "Let's go."

"But—"

"No questions," he hissed. "Now!"

Jake also stood and held up his hands, palms out. "Mr. Donatto, I—I…" he stammered.

"Shut up!" said the man, waving his finger at Jake's nose. "You just shut up!"

Angie started talking again, and this time Peter could hear the tightness in her throat. She was talking through gritted teeth. "Daddy," she said. "You're *embarrassing* me…"

The man said nothing. He looked around—at the stage, at the people staring at him, at McConnell— like someone who wasn't quite sure where he was. With his wide, bloodshot eyes and his shallow gasping breaths, the man looked like his heart might explode at any moment. Donatto glared at Jake, and then dragged his daughter away. She almost lost her balance, and her feet kicked up a spray of sand behind her. As they left, she turned and looked at Jake over her shoulder, reaching out with her free hand. Her mouth seemed to open as if she was going to say something, and then she melted into the darkness.

Jake slowly sat back down and turned toward Peter. "I hope I didn't get her in too much trouble," he said.

Peter frowned, tapping his finger against his chin. "I don't think it was you," he said. He caught a glimpse of his father. Nick Braddock was looking over at the Misfits, eyebrow raised. "Hmm," Peter said, "maybe it wouldn't hurt to take a look around." He surveyed the audience and the nearby stretch of beach. It seemed unlikely, Peter thought, that anyone would try to hurt McConnell tonight, in front of this large crowd, but why not take precautions? "I'll walk down that way," he said, pointing along the water's edge. "Jake, you take the other side. Mattie, you check out the area behind the stage."

"What do I do?" Byte asked.

Peter knocked against her cast with his knuckles. "You," he said, "get to enjoy the show."

The three separated, and as they walked off, Peter could hear Byte muttering to herself.

Mattie sighed as he trudged around to the back of the stage. He kept his eyes on the ground, careful not to step on the bright orange extension cords that ran from the stage all the way to the public restrooms, where they plugged into a six-outlet surge protector. From here he couldn't see the audience at all, just the huge amplifiers and a glimpse now and then of the back of Dylan McConnell's head. *Hmph,* he thought. *Just like Peter to stick me right in the thick of the action.* Some evil-looking waves lapped quietly against the shoreline. Maybe he should question them. A flock of seagulls—mighty suspicious, mind you—squawked and fluttered their wings nearby, looking for the tiny crumbs of sandwiches and cookies sunbathers had left in the sand. Maybe he should ask each bird to flash its ID.

He plopped down in the sand, pouting. Nothing was going on here. No one was anywhere near this area. The BPHS wood shop students who had built the stage used thin sheets of Masonite to mask off the front and sides, but they hadn't even bothered with the back. Mattie could look right underneath the platform and see the crisscrossed lengths of two-by-fours that served as bracing. See, he mused, even the builders hadn't thought that the area behind the stage was important.

Mattie paused. *What's that?*

Underneath the stage, not too far from the front, blinked a little pin-dot of red light. Mattie knew it had nothing to do with the stage equipment, so what could it be?

He lay down on his stomach and shimmied, snakelike, beneath the stage. He had to shoulder his way through the angled braces, occasionally cracking his head against a two-by-four. As he drew closer to the pin-dot of light, it grew larger, finally resolving into...*numerals?*

01:17...01:16...01:15...

Mattie could now make out the faint shape around the glowing numbers. He had seen enough movies to know he was looking at a bomb. His stomach flipped, and for a moment he thought he might throw up right there in the sand. The thing to do, of course, was to crawl out from beneath the platform, tell Mr. Braddock about the bomb, clear McConnell off the stage, and let the police evacuate the crowd.

All of which shouldn't take more than twenty minutes.

01:06...01:05...01:04...

Mattie whimpered but crawled forward, toward the bomb. He had no other choice. He scuttled past another brace, and then another, and was almost within arm's reach of the bomb when he felt a sharp jab in his rear end. He tried to move forward again, but something held him in place. A nail, hammered carelessly, had snagged the seat of his jeans. Mattie tried to pull away, but he only succeeded in twisting the fabric tighter around the nail.

00:49...00:48...00:47...

He reached out his hand as far as it would go, watched it quivering in the air less than a foot from the bomb. He shouted, but under all this wood, and with the blaring of the music above him, he knew no one could hear him.

Nick Braddock watched as Peter and Jake separated and began walking along the outer edges of the audience. They looked up and down each row, searching every face. A moment later Peter gazed for a very long time at the water's edge, and then at the endless line of lifeguard towers that stretched down the beach.

Nick watched them until they were almost out of sight, two faint shadows that finally melded into solid black. Whatever they were doing, they hadn't told him about it. Nor had they told any one of the half-dozen or so BPPD uniformed cops who'd been assigned to keep order tonight.

Nick drew in a deep breath and let it out in a long, hissing sigh. It could be nothing, he thought. On the other hand, someone had already tried to kill Dylan McConnell once—and had nearly killed Peter and his friends at the same time.

He strode over to Byte and knelt down next to her in the sand. "Is everything all right?" he asked.

She knew what he meant. She shot a look over her shoulder, in the general direction Jake had gone, and when she turned back to Nick, she crinkled her nose. The gesture, he thought, did not show a great depth of concern.

"Guess so," she said. "They're just looking around 'cause that guy was acting so weird." She reached for her crutches and started to haul herself to her feet. "Want some help?"

"No no no," Nick said, holding up a hand to stop her. "Don't get up. I'll look into it."

She can't get around very well if there's trouble, Nick thought. *Let her stay right up here next to the stage, where she'll be safe.*

00:24...00:23...00:22...

Mattie drew his knees in, braced his feet against one of the two-by-four supports, and pushed as hard as he could. He felt a terrible burning as the exposed nail cut across his rear end. He dug in harder, the wood creaking under his feet, and then he heard a great ripping sound and fell forward on his stomach. The air burst from his lungs in a loud *ooooff.*

00:17...00:16...00:15...

He rolled onto his back. The bomb was just above him, its digital readout faintly illuminating the explosive. It was brick-shaped, he noted, only smaller. Mattie had seen enough action movies to recognize it as some kind of plastique. Stuck inside the explosive was a steel pin, about three inches long and the width of a pencil. Two wires ran from this pin. One attached to the timer, and the other wrapped around the side of the bomb.

00:11...00:10...00:09...

The pin was clearly some kind of connector between the timer and the explosive. Mattie remembered the first *Die Hard* film—Bruce Willis foiling the bad guys by stealing some pins like these. They were a kind of mini-explosive, like really powerful firecrackers, designed to set off the plastique.

00:07...00:06...00:05...

Mattie's sweaty fingers gently tugged the pin from the waxlike brick. *That should do it,* he told himself. *It should be safe now, right?* Then, in a sudden flash, he remembered the detonator pin itself. It would be like a tiny grenade when it exploded, sending slivers of metal into his face and eyes. His hands flew to the wire connection and, once there, found a simple nine-volt battery. He tugged it from its connections. The timer dropped to **00:02,** stayed there an instant, then blinked out. The detonator pin hung over Mattie's nose, swinging like a tiny pendulum.

Mattie, too numb to think or feel, lay in the sand staring at the dangling pin, his chest rising and falling and his breath scraping the air.

Something was wrong.

Randy checked his watch a second time. He had synchronized it with the bomb's timer, and it told him the C4 should have turned into a fireball seconds ago. *Must have used a faulty detonator,* he thought.

He slowly unwrapped the towel from around the Winchester. He had wanted to avoid this—the bomb was so much less risky than hanging around to use a gun—but he recalled the newspaper article. McConnell would be talking to the FBI on Monday. The press would be crawling all over the man. Not even Bonhoffer could stop a new investigation.

He raised the rifle and peered through its scope at the stage. A head shot was out of the question—McConnell was too small a target at this distance. He would aim for the body, shoot *through* the guitar. Randy grimaced, held his breath, and curled his finger around the trigger.

McConnell closed his eyes, smiling as he sang. When the music was right, performing was like riding a raft on a gentle river. Peaceful. Easy. It carried him along, and it was no effort at all to take an audience with him.

Then, with no warning, his guitar imploded. The tension from the steel strings blew it inward, sending out a cloud of splinters and a spray of wire. It busted clean in two, right at the joint of the neck and body. McConnell flicked his head to the side and felt the broken strings scratch his face.

At the same time, he heard a loud boom echoing from down the beach. Someone was shooting at him. Again.

He heard another boom, and a chunk of wood splintered up from the stage floor. McConnell dove behind an amplifier. Someone in the audience began to scream.

Where was Peter?

Jake was walking behind the audience, eyeing the rows closest to the parking area, when he heard the first shot.

Peter was on the opposite side, walking in the moist sand that marked the shoreline. They had been able to see each other, even wave to each other, only moments ago. Then Jake heard the first loud boom come from the lifeguard tower that stood perhaps a hundred yards down the beach. He saw a tongue of flame burst from the structure's tiny side window. When the rifle boomed a second time, Jake dove to the sand, rolling until he felt the ground beneath him turn into the hard concrete of the walkway. Once there, he lay still, his body flat against the parking lot asphalt and hidden somewhat behind a curb. He heard screaming behind him. Dozens of people were fleeing, shrieking, holding their hands around their heads as they ran in the dark toward their cars. Others, he saw, rolled onto their stomachs in the sand. Some fled to the water.

Jake thought of Byte in her clunky cast and those crutches she still hadn't quite mastered. He thought of Mattie struggling to help her. The policemen had drawn their weapons, aware of the gunfire, but they were looking around at all the confusion—the screaming, the running—and they couldn't see where the shots had originated. Jake considered standing up and waving his arms, shouting "Over there! The gunman is in the tower!" Then he decided he might just as well stand up holding a sign for the gunman saying, "Shoot me, please!"

Where was Peter?

From out of the darkness, a shadow came toward Jake. It seemed less like a man than like some horrible animal.

It shuffled toward him, snorting and growling, a great horn rising from its head. He watched it stagger forward on two legs, while a separate pair of legs appeared to drag in the sand. It drew closer, and Jake cowered even lower against the ground.

Then the animal stepped out of the shadows cast by the lifeguard tower and into the pale moonlight. The animal, Jake saw, was a man. The snorting he had heard was in fact the man's desperate breathing, a deep sucking in of air followed by a whimper. The growls were the man's mutterings. The great horn was the barrel of a rifle slung across the man's back and pointing upward.

The other pair of legs belonged to Peter.

Jake understood now what had happened to his friend. Before the shooting started, Peter must have drifted ahead of Jake, approaching the lifeguard tower where the man was hiding. In the darkness, and with the narrow view provided by the window, the man had not seen Peter until it was too late. Jake imagined the gunman clattering down the tower's steel ladder, eager to make his escape, and perhaps slamming right into Peter as he did. Jake could now see the man's thick arm wrapped around Peter's neck, dragging Peter with him. The man gripped a revolver, which he held jammed against Peter's temple. Peter's eyeglasses were askew, one earpiece bent and pointing down at his chin.

"You thought I didn't recognize you," the man muttered. "But I know who you are. I know your name." He did not focus on Peter as he spoke. Instead his eyes were wide and yellow in the moonlight, flickering here and there. His face glistened with sweat. "So you be quiet," the man went on. "Or I'll kill you—kill your friends."

As he watched, Jake's heart began to pound. The man spun around, swinging Peter around with him, and froze. His eyes narrowed, and he stopped his muttering.

The revolver swung away from Peter's head and pointed at Jake. "You!" the man shouted. "Get up! I know who you are too."

Jake rose to his feet, his palms extended to show they were empty. *This guy's desperate; he's insane.* Jake imagined Dylan McConnell face down on the stage, bleeding. And who got the second bullet? Mattie? Byte? Were the policemen at the concert running toward him now with their weapons drawn, or were they tending the wounded? He wanted to look back at the stage, but he didn't dare. He listened for sirens but heard none. The gunman glanced at the stage, at the parking lot, at him. He could tell what the man was thinking—hold on to his hostage, or free Peter and make a mad dash for his car? The man seemed incapable of deciding. His breathing grew shallower and more labored, and his teeth bit deeply into his lower lip.

Maybe, Jake thought, *I can slow the guy down even more by adding to the confusion.* "I know who you are too," Jake lied. "You might as well turn yourself in, before anyone else gets hurt." Then, as if to prove that he wasn't lying, Jake added, "Remember Trenton State? April 11, 1970?"

Uh oh.

As soon as the words came out, Jake knew he had gone too far. Instead of further confusing the man, Jake had only made him more desperate. The man swung around, bellowing and hurling Peter into the sand. His gun hand swept in an arc with no hint of hesitation or confusion. It pointed at Jake. The man's thumb clicked back the gun's hammer, and Jake could almost sense the finger tightening against the trigger.

An instant later, the air vibrated with the echo of gunfire. *Blam! Blam! Blam!*

Jake flinched at the noise, expecting three lead pellets, small and white-hot, to crash into his ribs. When they never arrived, he looked up to see the gunman teetering like a dead tree whose roots had shriveled. Three red spots stood out on the man's chest. They grew larger, expanding until their edges met and blended. Soon they became one large spot, stretching from the man's upper chest to the top of his huge silver belt buckle. The gunman, whoever he was, fell forward, dead.

Jake turned. Several yards away, crouched behind a car for cover, was Peter's father. Nick Braddock held his gun at arm's length, both hands cradling it for accuracy. Wisps of smoke trailed from the gun's barrel.

"You all right?" Nick asked.

"I'm fine, Dad," said Peter. He stood, brushing the sand from his face and clothing. Jake, however, found he couldn't speak. He just looked at Mr. Braddock and nodded. A moment later, three BPPD uniformed officers came running up with guns drawn, and Mr. Braddock flashed them his FBI credentials.

Jake sat down in the sand. Behind him, shrill in the clear night air, came the wail of sirens.

Peter, Jake, and Mr. Braddock returned to find Dylan McConnell sitting on the edge of the stage. Byte sat next to him, fingering the neck of his shattered guitar. Most of the concertgoers had fled, Peter saw, but a few still huddled in groups, whispering to one another.

"Everyone okay?" Peter asked.

Byte nodded. "You catch the guy?"

"Yes," said Mr. Braddock.

He said nothing more, and Peter felt a rush of relief. He didn't much feel like telling the whole story either. Byte seemed to be staring at his nose, and he hurriedly set his broken glasses straight.

"Hey," said Jake, frowning, "where's Mattie?"

Just as he spoke, Mattie wandered from behind the stage. His hair looked matted, and sand lay in flecks across his face and clothing. Several police officers stood behind the stage, huddling over something.

"Too bad you missed out on all the action," said Jake. For some reason Peter did not understand, Mattie picked up a discarded soft drink cup and hurled it at them.

"Can we just go home, please?" Mattie asked.

"Sure," said Mr. Braddock.

"Good." Mattie spun around and headed for the parking lot, clearly determined to be first in the car.

Byte laughed. "Hey, Mattie," she called. "Um—nice butt."

Mattie reached behind and gripped the torn seat of his pants, holding it in place. "Shut up," he said.

"What is that?" Jake asked. "Are you going for, like, a grunge look or something?"

"*I said shut up.*"

epilogue

Peter leaned back in the wooden chair, his eyes closed and his face angled toward the ceiling. He heard the library door open, so with a great effort of will he lifted his head and pried one eye open. As he suspected, Jake and Mattie had entered and were approaching his table. Both boys moved a little like Frankenstein's monster. Jake's shirttail had pulled out on one side, and he either hadn't noticed or didn't care. Mattie's shoelaces were undone, and he *galumphed* across the floor.

When they arrived at the table, however, all three boys grinned. Jake held his palm out, and Peter slapped it in victory. Next Jake held the palm up for Mattie—far higher than Mattie's reach—and Mattie feigned a high five, waving at empty air.

The door opened again, and Byte entered. She planted her crutches and swung her legs through them in a way that reminded Peter of chimpanzees walking on their knuckles. He decided, even through his brain's early morning fog, that he would remain much healthier if he never told her that.

As she drew closer, Peter could see she had pulled her hair into a ponytail. On her cheek were faint red lines where she had pressed her face into her pillow.

Mattie looked at her. "Hey, remember *Night of the Living Dead?*" he asked. "That movie about all those zombie corpses walking around?"

Byte nodded.

Mattie hesitated. "Oooohh, never mind," he said, slinking into his chair. "Something just made me think of it."

Ignoring the comment, Byte leaned her crutches against a chair and threw her arms around Jake's neck. "We did it," she whispered. Peter leaned over, and she hugged him just as hard and just as long. Finally, she turned and glared at Mattie. "All right," she said, and the glare faded into a smile. "You too. C'mere, you little bug." For some reason, Mattie got the longest hug of all—maybe, Peter decided, because he had believed in McConnell all along.

For the next few moments, the Misfits remained silent. Last night's board meeting had been scheduled from 7:00 to 9:00, but by 11:30 the shouting had just gotten started. Over a hundred people—parents, teachers, students—had shown up to voice their opinions about the book banning. Ms. Langley spoke for five solid minutes without interruption, and the crowd had stood, applauding when she finished. Peter grinned at the memory—not at the speech or the applause, but at the purple tinge on Steadham's face.

They had won. By a four to three vote, the board had agreed to return the banned books to the library.

As Peter mulled these thoughts, a hand reached past his shoulder and rapped its knuckles on the library table. "Anybody home?" asked a woman's voice.

"Ms. Langley!" cried Byte. "Are you back?"

The librarian slid a chair over and joined them at the table. "That's still a yes-no-maybe," she said. She waggled her hand back and forth, as though weighing the probabilities. Then she smiled. "Let's just say it's looking good."

For some strange reason, Peter found himself wishing that Ms. Langley had a pencil tucked behind her ear or clenched between her teeth. She never seemed to have a place for that pencil while she was working, and Peter would have found some comfort in seeing it now. "Well," he said, "you'll at least be back next year, right? I mean, you have to be here when we graduate…"

The librarian gazed at each of them. "You haven't heard then," she said quietly.

"Heard what?" Jake asked.

Ms. Langley leaned back in her chair. The index finger of her right hand drummed against the tabletop. "Mr. Steadham," she said, "has resigned. He'll be leaving at the end of the year." She shrugged. "I'm two credits shy of earning my administrative credential, so I thought I'd take a night class at the university and maybe apply for the job. What do you say? Think I'd make a good principal?"

"You'd be *awesome*," said Mattie. "Can I have your electric pencil sharpener?"

"Nope," said Ms. Langley.

Peter and Jake beamed—Ms. Langley would be a *great* principal. Byte said nothing, but Peter saw the way she set her elbows against the tabletop and rested her chin in her hands. She was smiling so broadly he doubted she could have said anything even if she'd wanted to.

"I have to run," said Ms. Langley. "Some business at the district office." She rose and placed her hands on Byte's shoulders, squeezing them gently. Then she turned away. The Misfits watched her leave, even watched the library door swing closed behind her.

"Hey…Peter?"

It was Mattie. The youngest Misfit stared down at the table. He had taken his deck of "magic" cards from its box and was absently riffling their edges. Peter, of course, knew what his friend was going to ask even before Mattie began. It was, after all, the only question the Misfits hadn't answered. "What about Mr. McConnell? Do you know what's going to happen to him?"

Peter shook his head. After spending hours yesterday with McConnell, his lawyer, and the U.S. Attorney, Nick Braddock had come home silent as a stone.

Later that evening, Peter found his dad kneeling in front of the small stone fireplace in his study. Nick Braddock was taking sheets of newspaper and crumpling them into balls. Next to him sat a brass holder containing three heavy pine logs and, nearby, a canvas carrier stuffed with kindling. Peter shrugged out of his light jacket and laid it across the back of a chair. *A fire?* The room already felt a little warm.

As Peter watched, his father took up another sheet of newspaper. The FBI agent remained silent, scowling as he crushed the sheet into a tight ball. He then set the paper aside and stared at his hands, which were blackened by the newsprint. He squeezed his eyes shut, and the scowl on his face grew deeper.

"Dad?"

His father smiled weakly and patted the carpet next to him. "Sit down here and give me a hand."

Peter knelt next to his father and began crumpling newspaper as well. When they had seven or eight pieces, they set them in rows in the fireplace to serve as a bed for the kindling. Next they piled on dry twigs, and then some thicker cuttings from dead branches.

"That's right," said Nick. "Quick-burning stuff on the bottom. How was school today?"

"Fine," said Peter. The kindling looked perfect. He and his father each grabbed a log and set it across the andirons.

"Ms. Langley coming back?"

"Looks like it."

Peter wanted to blurt out his question, but he sensed that his father wanted to tell him about McConnell in his own way. Mr. Braddock took a long wooden fireplace match, struck it against the stone, and touched it to the balls of newspaper. They turned black and curled into tiny flakes of ash, their flames crackling around the dry twigs.

"Dad—?" asked Peter.

"Brought some work home," said Mr. Braddock flatly. "Thought I'd do it here." He jabbed at the logs with a poker, leaving more space between them so that oxygen could feed the flames. "You're welcome to take a look at it." His voice sounded almost robotlike.

Peter then looked at the thick file folder sitting in his father's open briefcase on the desk. The tab at the top of the folder said McConnell, Dylan. He picked up the file and flipped through its contents. What he discovered there made his stomach sink—a detailed report on the bombing at Trenton State. Peter swallowed. It was the whole story, everything from the original investigation in 1970 through the later cover-up. With this evidence, everyone involved could go to jail.

On the top sheet was a Post-It note with a hastily scrawled message. It said, "Nick, it's yours now. I know you'll do the right thing." The initials at the bottom of the note said "P.B." Paul Bonhoffer.

The words of the note stared up at Peter. *The right thing.* What exactly had Bonhoffer meant? Was it right to put Dylan McConnell in jail now, thirty years after his crime? Was it right for Bonhoffer to lose his FBI credentials? Was it right to jail Mr. Donatto—and leave Angela without a father? The Vietnam War was a time when good people, in good conscience, did bad things. On Luna's film, Peter had seen protesters hurling rocks and setting pipe bombs. He had seen National Guardsmen shotting unarmed demonstrators. And just weeks ago, at his own school, Peter had seen students who rarely broke rules setting off false fire alarms and refusing to attend class.

Nick Braddock's voice interrupted Peter's thoughts. "Let me see that."

Nick took the file from Peter's hand and gazed at the top sheet for a very long time. He slipped the sheet from the folder, turned, and without a word set it atop the burning logs. The edges of the paper turned a glowing red, then black. A dark spot formed in the center of the sheet and expanded outward toward the edges. An instant later, the paper was gone.

Peter reached for the next sheet himself. If his father was going to do this he would not do it alone. Peter stared at his dad, almost daring the agent to stop him.

"Nice night for a fire, huh?" Nick asked.

Peter nodded and fed the sheet into the flames.

OTHER BOOKS IN THE MISFITS, INC. SERIES

MISFITS, INC. NO. 1: The Vanishing Chip
(1-56145-176-2 • $5.95)
In their first case, the Misfits band together to clear Mattie's grandfather, who stands falsely accused of stealing a million-dollar computer chip from a local museum.

MISFITS, INC. NO. 2: Of Heroes and Villains
1-56145-178-9 • $5.95)
In their second case, the Misfits are mysteriously summoned to a comic book convention, where a comic book villain seems to come to life to commit a daring crime. When the Misfits attempt to solve the crime, they discover that someone close to them may be involved in the heist.

MISFITS, INC. NO. 3: Growler's Horn
(1-56145-206-8 • $5.95)
What does the note found in Jake's clarinet mean about the disappearance of a jazz musician and three million dollars? In their third case, the Misfits are driven to unravel the secret of Growler's horn, attempting to restore the good name of an innocent man.

MISFITS, INC. NO. 4: The Kingfisher's Tale
(1-56145-226-2 • $5.95)
When the Misfits explore the national forest near Byte's family cabin, they discover several dead endangered kingfisher birds, and suddenly find themselves in the middle of a terrifying ecological mystery and a looming political scandal.